Victor M. Vita

Poems of the Future

Vol. 1

Victor M. Vita

Poems of the Future
Vol. 1

ISBN/EAN: 9783337408688

Printed in Europe, USA, Canada, Australia, Japan

Cover: Foto ©Andreas Hilbeck / pixelio.de

More available books at **www.hansebooks.com**

POEMS OF THE FUTURE.

BY

VICTOR M. VITA,

VOL. I.

LONDON:
ARTHUR H. MOXON, 12 TAVISTOCK STREET,
COVENT GARDEN.

———

1879.

DEDICATION.

TO

POSTERITY:—AND MY SISTER.

DEDICATORY.

My sister!   Soul who art brother of my soul,
Whose love is more than sister's love to mine,
The best I have known, the truest to console,
First to respond, and deepest to divine ;
Who hast soothed my wounds so oft with oil ; with
     wine
Restored my spirit ; whose bright sympathy
Has beckoned forth my dreams, to play with thine—
The only dreams spared by reality,
My mocker else—those dreams here do I pledge to thee.

These first-fruits of my thoughts—(thoughts that
     before
I gave them to the world, I gave to thee,
Who canst interpret by supplying more
Than my words say, knowing how imperfectly
They speak, knowing I mean more than words may be
Adequate to suggest ; who hast sent to meet
The feeble utterance of these thoughts, to me
Return more precious, thoughts *unuttered* sweet—
In perfect comprehension)—these lay I at thy feet.

In tribute of the young ideals fair
Mutual, which we did long since consecrate
Unto each other ; in the hope to share
Yet their blest influence ; do I dedicate—
—Ignoring what be their desert, their fate—
These to thy name. Would it might ever be
I could immortalise it—make it great—
Let its remembrance lovely as to me
Be unto others : *then* my songs were worthy thee.

All through thy life, which up to mine has grown,
Since I was child, thou little sister child,
Thou hast my heart's one passionate secret known—
Yea, even familiar with its ravings wild
Hast learned to fear them not ; but solaced mild
With intimate counsel, with companion aid,
—Won me to tame my frenzy, reconciled
My force to its subdual ; and, final, made
Free outlet for it when it could no more be stayed.

O ! If, as I accept thy prophecy
Of future and of fame for me, I could
Be but inspired to give true augury
Of thy life, thou accepting it :—I would
(Heaven seal my reading of it !)—all the good
Of earth's gift, all the beautiful of its waste
Put to thy portion ;—for thy maidenhood
Be love, in all its fulness. *I* would taste
Bliss by mere sips, then pass it on to thee in haste.

All the delights that I have held so light—
For charm of change, for curiosity,

CONTENTS.

TRIONFO.

THE great, full moment is arrived for me
To which my being hath tended, with its whole
Endowments, its complete capacity,
Since it hath felt intensity of soul,
And recognised its power to outward fling
The impulses that through its inmost roll,
The shocks that move its depths, the potent swing
Of subtlest instincts of identity
Into the universal ; learnt to bring
All motions of the lesser life, the free
Utterances of the individual will
Within the scope of the grand unity
Which sways all diverse thoughts and actions still,
Linking them, each in infinitesimal place,
In one unbroken order, to fulfil
The plan complete moulded of infinite space,
Infrangible, imperturbable. To thee
Who hast spanned the cycles of Time's goalless race,
Felt the impalpable throb of harmony
Through the chaotic void, with its dull roar
Of world's confusion, of life's destiny,
Its deafening whirr, its rush for evermore
From change to change of purposelessness vain,

A

Its rocking speed, its sudden spasms quick o'er,
Its deathly lapse to impotence inane,
Its dull, cold, heavy torpidness, its start
Of grim recoil convulsive : with disdain
Tearing all bonds, all boundaries apart,
Precipitating thyself unguided, lone,
In awful formlessness ;—to thee, who art,
O spirit most mystical, of might unknown,
Shivering through my mortality, dread-rife,
I have strained and striven ; and to thee alone,
O spirit most wonderful, genius of life,
I stretch, with absolute trust, my wide desire,
That vivifies itself through constant strife,
By being fixed on thy swift flight ; the higher
Thou soarest, yet the more I feel for thee,
And cling after thy shadow, and aspire
With agonising, with sick ecstasy,
With pangs of rapturous pain, most faint and keen,
Most sharp and languishing.   O, when shall be
The moment of attainment ? when I lean
Panting against the pillar for bound-mark set
Of the conquered ages ?   What is, what hath been,
Hath it such term ?   O glory of life !   And yet
So bitter hath been my seeming endless cry,
Throughout my search—O long, O long regret !—
To find such glory ; at least, or ere I die
To look on its assurance, or to dwell
A moment in its belief.   O why, O why
Is it incompatible with life, as well
As with death's horrible extinction ?   Nay,
Life is so long, too long, yet may not tell
The triumph which should take its shame away :

Surely, for that, at last, it was create ;
Its ultimate meaning, surely, therein lay—
O weary cry ! O wrestling long with fate,
Shall it be baffled ?   No ; there fall on me
From gloom to gloom of this my shadowy state
Whisper-like gleamings, portents of to be,
Shaking my weak heart with inspiring thrill,
With strength of instantaneous certainty.
O strength, refresh thyself ! Falter not, will !
It must be given thee ; that thou seek'st is thine,
That object only which thy wish shall fill,
That perfect union with the source divine
Of Life's eternal secret. . . .   Ah, most dear,
Most exquisite glory of existence—Mine !
I feel it now—the moment grand is here.
Moment of my foreboding : it must be
My everlasting faith, my love sincere,
My earnestness, receives its crown : on me
Fulness of knowledge pours, passing all sense.
It seems the eve of my eternity, . . .
The inexpressible calm, the bliss intense,
The satisfaction finished, the delight
Of strifeless, timeless peace, would whelm me.   Hence
Disturbing phantoms of my soul's past night,
Ye restless heavings of my troubled thought,
Stings of my single griefs—ye have no right
To mar my spirit's placidity—as ought
More than the stirs ruffling the stable sea ;
The swells that near its surface sweep—are nought ;
And nought are my own life-thrills unto me,
Save that with pain I feel them quiver slight
Below the oneness vast, the entirety

Of all life-movement.   The pure flood of light
Anon must break into reflections fleet
In flashing on my self-hood ; . . .   but the sight
That passes o'er such breaks with patience meet,
Shall soon behold unhindered, fearlessly,
Only the utter brightness—in one sheet
Of dazzling light, of perfect purity.

TRAGEDY FRAGMENTS.

THE END.

(Soliloquy by a Desperado on the Eve of Suicide.)

HERE must I pause, in the tempestuous rush
In which Life's forces dire have plunged my soul.
Here against Life at last I make revolt,
And take my stand, O thou more pitying,
More equal power, here before *thee*, O Death !
My burdened spirit flees for refuge here
Unto thee, with its overwhelming charge
Of questions awful and importunate.
O, I must have the answer ! *answer* me !
Answer ! O answer, answer ! All these years
I have cried to Life, in vain ; and now, to thee
I cry, O answer ! Death ! O, answer me !

I have used my prowess to its utmost pitch ;
My strength is all exhausted ; it hath done
Great things :—hath met in fierce attack the might
Of passion, and hath overcome ; hath borne
The onslaught of a thousand ills combined—
Grief, disappointment, envy—even remorse ;
Hath vanquished *Fear :* that foe should be the last,
For utterly my energies are spent,
And my last weapon is lost.   I stand alone
All feeble, and disarmed, the final shock

To encounter, with the adversary dread,
The last, the unconquerable one—Despair.
Now must I look in my opponent's face,
And without quarter fall ; else, quailing, pray
For terms, and shamefully surrender ; else
Flee, and be henceforth hunted through the world
By the triumphant vanquisher, whom once
I had boasted I would meet, and in fair field
Wrestle with manfully.　Fair field, alas !
May unto mortals ne'er accorded be
In the tremendous combat that they wage
With all the powers of Destiny.　But, so,—
I have fought my fight, and poured my blood in vain.
I will not soil my colours in retreat ;
Into the face I look Despair ; I stand
Before the tyrant—not resisting—not
Desisting ; with indifference, to receive
The last blow.　Still audacious, I will die.

Yes. . . .　I have struggled free of soul, and felt
Contempt of men, in their traditions bound.
O fatal freedom !　Let one planet be
Released from its inevitable law
Of gravitation, guide compulsory—
Who, then, or what, should be accountable
For the wide path opened unto it in space ?
Were there not infinite opportunity
For the new sweep of a limitless career ?
How were it with that planet ?　Would it not
Be shattered into atoms helplessly ?—
And I as helpless.　Whither shall I go
Now I have left the safe track, circumscribed

By the old bounds set up in pathless space?
Is it my fault that their compulsion failed?
If they were law, why then not absolute?
Why not escapeless, once imposed on me,
And constant? How can that, which lets itself
Be scorned, rejected with impunity,
Claim our inviolable allegiance?
And, failing that, charge us with sacrilege
Who thus do break its bonds? Is it *Heaven's* gift,
Reason? which, by its use—or even abuse
Possible, with the gift unto our charge
Committed—bears on the resistless soul
By its sheer force away, *away* from Heaven?
So far. . . . . O! should we ever find it true,
That once beloved, now vanished myth of Heaven,
Might we not curse it for this godlike gift,
Seductive thus to poor humanity? . . .
Who would not seek out Heaven? Who would not love
With every faculty of mind and heart
God, were it realisable? as we all
Have loved it once, in its sublime idea. . . . .
But, to be thus misled—if *this* be sin,
'Tis arbitrary as the punishment.

O! I have found it *is* a fearful thing
To be without God in the world. God!—God!
Long after all the sweet and hallowed hopes
Laid by religion round that sacred name
To guard it from assailment rude, had fled,
The blessed spell of memory clung to it,
And, with a mighty power, warded from it
All profanation. I have bowed before

That idol—yea, and done it solemn rites
With reverent homage,—when I long had ceased
To hold belief in its fond efficacy—
For the mere love I bore its loveliness.
I have paid worship to its presence in awe,
Constrained by my strong yearning to the ideal
Which unto others, in their simple faith,
Yielded implicit satisfaction.   Well
Had I not lost that faith ; for I have gained
No substitute—and learned to look for none.
This is the curse—*Without God in the world.*
O ! better—it were better to be out,
Out into all the horrors of the Unknown,
Than thus, unknowing, with untamed desire
To know, be ceaseless menaced by the vague
Unanswerable terrorism of dreams ;
Tantalised with hallucinations ; mocked
By fictions of the unstable consciousness ;
Humiliated by the pauseless strife
Of reason and unreason in the soul.

If there is not a God, who rules by laws
To which men's actions, either by the sure
Penalty of infraction manifest,
  Or by obedience, must submit themselves,
Then there is *Fate* ; who rules, however blind,
Purposeless, and malign as despots rule ;
And just as sure, men's actions, unto her
Either submissive or rebellious vain,
Are subject to her sway.—Yes, there is Fate ;—
A most ironic arbitress, who laughs

When men, embarassed by two meeting paths
Lying before their way unclear, choose one
In a chance moment—one uncertain step
Take, and are evermore condemned to go
Through the by-path misleading ; following out
Its cursed intricacies, severed far
And hopelessly from the desired highway
Which leads through life so even, unopposed
By obstacles that throng the ravines deep
Through which the tangled, devious by-paths stray.
Who are they, who can find their way direct,
And keep it unconfused ?   The privileged
On whom, in her caprice, Fate showers her gifts.
The wariest, else, must stumble and be lost.
Yes, there is Fate ; who laughs convulsively
When daring hands make rash experiment—
Seizing some poisoned cup, perchance, to try,
In sport of curiosity, the effect
Of its intoxication momentary—
In a few instants is the risk repaid ;
The proof has stood, the effervescence brief
Is over, . .   but its work of gradual blight
Remains in perpetuity ; a force
Inscrutable dwells in it, and doth course
Into the blood, tainting it evermore,
Transforming its vitality, with bane
All ineradicable.—Life is full
Of such insidious poisons :   O the lips
Steeped in them, nnsuspectingly ! the hearts
Scathed with their deathless burning !   O the souls
That writhe in lingering throes of that slow pain
Drunk long since in the draught of reckless play !

So have *I* been deluded and accursed ;
So have *I* been entangled in my doom.

My strength of thought has been of no avail
To guide my actions in the complex web
Of opportunity, of consequence,
Of chance, of impulse and of circumstance.
My will, that once hath given the impetus—
Unwitting oft—to some swift shaft of Fate
Hath no more power to interrupt its course,
Or check its speed.   Were all our lots ordained,
And all apparent inconsistency
Reducible to arbitrary plan ;—
However harsh and ruthless be the law
By which undeviatingly were held
All our forced actions, *that* at least could be
Indisputably fixed, and recognised,
And by its victims contemplated : then,
With stolid resignation, or proud calm,
We could endure, and wait ; give up, and rest.
Or, were the conduct of our destiny
Given into our own hands, might we choose out
What means we would, and mould them as we pleased,
And guide their forces, and direct their strength ;
Might we but undeceived once calculate
The impending train of one deliberate act,
The ancestry of but one moment's whim,
The progress of one motion from its start,
The tendency of one development
To its conclusion : then we need not shrink
To take upon ourselves in its full weight
Our duty of responsibility ;

Then might we judge, and ponder ; think and dare ;
Accept the ultimate issues of our deeds
Whether they be good or evil ; expiate
With careless courage—negligence, or ill,
Or self-inflicted wrong. Whate'er might be
Our errors, and the sufferings they entailed,
To all of these were reason reconciled.
But 'tis this contradiction cynical
In the eternal order, that thus moves
To passionate complaint the goaded soul.
'Tis this fortuitous, counteracting law,
This horrible constraint of liberty,
Sarcastic freedom of necessity ;
This stern compulsion of mere accident ! . . .

Since I have failed to learn the logic of Life,
To thee I turn, O Death ! and do appeal
To thee, to teach me thine. I have taught myself
(In sheer despair of finding compromise
Midst multitudious systems that compete
For acceptation, to account for all
The anomalies, all the perversities
Of moral order ; in despair to prove
Consistency in any principle,
Or, in its application feasible
Universality) *this* axiom
Agnostic. O ! the lesson has been hard,
And in my heart's blood have I written it,
And with my life will I its record seal,
So earnest am I, though so impious—
There is no right: . . . . . .

. . . . Therefore, *There is no wrong.*

And is this all? All that rewards the years
Snatched from world's pleasures, and pure, innocent
    joys,
Unto the quest of this forbidden fruit,
This knowledge madly thirsted for? Is this
All that redeems the fury unexpressed
Of the protracted anguish of those hours
Which I have sacrificed—alas! in vain!—
To the fierce ardour of my longing soul
Absorbed in its inquiry? *Is this all?*
Yes: all! Now have I carried my research
As far as it is possible within
The limits of this life. Now I have tried
All the experiments within the reach
Of my command: but none was final. Now
I *will* thwart those blind forces that may be
In chance collusion to drag on my life
Into their possible contingencies
Of combination. I will interfere
And break their continuity; withdraw
As individual, from the mingling mass
In rash confusion, chaos general.
At least I will, by voluntary act,
Draw in the reins with tight and vigorous clutch,
Curbing, by will, my life's fatuitous course.

O Death! To thee, at last, I bring my plaint.
For the full play of my soul's powers, I demand
A new beginning—Or if not—*The End.*

ENDLESS.

I MUST submit.   Rebellion is in vain.
Solemn renewal there hath now been made
Of the compact whereby I am bound to Life.
I dared to deem the period was nigh
Of the expiration of its terms, whereon
I might demand, at my own choice, release ;
But I have knelt before the throne of Death
And in that presence-chamber, lowly bowed,
Proffered my bold request ; and solemnly
Have been refused, and with reproach abashed ;
And at Death's awful hands have taken back
My life as gift.   I know that I must live :
I may not look for respite speedy now
From these responsibilities, which I
Myself, these cares which adversaries fierce
Have wound about me.   I must break through all
To clear for my tired feet a little path
Where I may walk along, encumbered not
By the tangle that has long been gathering round
Through my own desperation, my neglect.
How fain would I lie down awhile, and sleep !
Throw off, as with a dream, the weary load
Of my accumulation of regrets ;
Wake up, and find my life lie all spread out
Before me, to begin anew, to form
Its future course, unfettered by restraints
Of the obligations of my long-mourned past !
Would that retaliation e'er might be
Exhausted ; would that consequence were spent !

Idle the wish! I must take up again
The thread I had cast down impatiently—
Must ravel it out, and work it to the end.
Ah! Rest shall come at last! And now and then
There will be time to turn my thoughts away
From the bewildering of their changeful throes,
And fix them peaceful on that solace blest.
Death, in his own good time, at his sweet will,
Shall cancel all these cruel bonds ; shall make
Me like to my surroundings ;—all alike
Patient, and mute, guiltless and passionless.
And sometimes, thinking on that certainty
I feel no more the present sting of life ;
(Sin is that sting—the sting of *life*, not *death*)
I feel already what the soothing calm
Of sure annihilation works for all.
Nay, oft am I astonished, in the midst
Of a wild paroxysm possessing me,
When the ungovernable force of thoughts
In rashest strife, crowding on memory,
Has left my reason breathless to sustain
The shock of those unintermittent darts,
Wherewith they goad—ah! not to madness—worse,
To the mad longing for madness as relief—
When I have flung myself upon the ground
In furious inanition, in revolt
At the impotent confusion that doth rage
Of all the passions in their conflict dire :
Then, in that conflict's forced and helpless pause,
Sudden a chill fit falls upon my heart ;
I start, as one who finds he beats the air ;
I gasp, as one who with returning sense

Sees the last phantasm of a fading dream
Identify itself with some unstrange
Remembered object in his waking life.
The disillusion seems complete and clear ;
It seems that I am my old self no more,
That a new self is possible to me,
Disimplicated from my cursèd chains,
My thraldom of the present and the past.
It seems that all my griefs are griefs no more—
Almost as though they never had been mine.
It seems as though the horrible thoughts, so long
My close companions, were called up at will,
And might be wantonly dismissed ; it seems
My very woes are all imaginary,
My sadness is but feigned.   Then I arise,
With a strange feeling—it is not of strength,
But like to the forebodings of faint strength
In one who rises from a long, deep trance,
And feels his way uncertainly, and tries
To call to him his former consciousness,
To make it tally with the impressions new
Of the regifted sense ; and springs to life,
And staggers, but half-recovered, dizzily.
To me comes, in such moments, dim desire
To go forth, a new man, into the world,
And drink with feverish haste some draught of joy.
But the old numbness steals on me apace,
The old bewildered sense of pain ; the old
Despairing apathy reclaims me soon. . . . . .
Such is the life I have to look unto—
Such I accept it.   I have ceased to cry,
Ceased to undo, to struggle, to lament :

I live, and know my own heart's bitterness.
How often have I sought to challenge death,
And sought in vain.   Like to that king, who tried
In youth all poisons, so that when he would
Their aid, to end his weariness, it failed—
I have to danger so inured myself
That all the efforts of my hardihood
Have finally been baffled.   I have found
It boots me not to seek an earlier end,
Than for my charmed life in some future waits.
Then, I have given myself sweet flattery ;
Said that I must be by God's will reserved
For some great deed to do, some goodness yet
Whose service may retrieve my wasted soul.
It must be that I am observed by Heaven,
And kept for holy purpose ; it must be
That I am destined for whate'er, henceforth,
Shall complicate, by seeming chance, my lot.
There must be yet some meaning in my life ;
There must be hope for me ;—must be some power
Left in me, to develop for world's weal.
My spirit, trampled down in sin and grief
Shall yet be raised ; its vindication yet
Shall be acknowledged by the Lord of life. . . .
And, when that ecstasy has died away,
I seek for satisfaction from myself,
And find, in newer guise, that which I sought
In death, now in that search I have been foiled.
The old, vain, fervent, passionate desire
For immortality, has now recoiled
Upon the love of life.   I thought before,
I had no love of life : I never longed

For the happiness that it was life's to give,
Ere I had forfeited my claim to it.
I shut my eyes upon the offerings fair
Wherewith life tempts life-lovers : I would none
Of such delusions ; but the life beyond,
Whose beauty all was in stability,
And yet whose dearest charm was mystery,
Whose very being was but of belief—
For that would I have once given all beside !
But that dear yearning shamefully was mocked :
For my renunciation of earth's bliss
Heaven rendered me—only blank doubt ; returned
To my wild prayers for affirmation, but
A cold, derisive, iterated—*No.*
I can recal even now the shock, the thrill,
Of that first whelm of anguish, when I found
Myself by God abandoned, left a prey
To the clamour of my own heart's questionings
Unanswerable ; I could not deaf myself
To the awful execrations of the voice
That echoed God's negation in my soul.
Then did I, fierce and desperate, dash myself
Into life's pleasures ;—caring not for ought
(It was too late ? for all capacity
Of joyousness through my stern toil was gone
But vowing in defiance, I would snatch
By force some recompense for broken trust.
Unholiness should yield me some return
For holiness deceived. . . . Too well, too well
The world responded to my mad demand.
Its pleasures, that I thought to take by storm
And sacrifice to my indifference

With scornful pride, came surely at my call ;
Came, and avenged themselves on me ; o'ercame
And then betrayed me ; lured me in their toils,
Made me fast captive, then deserted me.
And yet in my deep pain I almost dare
Rejoice that I lost *first* my hopes of Heaven ;
That it was not through late distrust of men
I learnt to cast away all faith in God :—
That had been fearfuller.   And yet, perhaps,
Had it not been that I had let go faith,
And hope, and prayer, and trust in heavenly love,
They might have saved me, when the danger came
In which I had no help, and so succumbed.
The seaman, who, in sport or heedlessness,
Loses his rudder while the sea is calm,
And recks not of his loss—must rue it soon,
Proving his need, when comes the ruthless storm
And shatters his frail craft.   So I went down
In such a storm, that many another man,
Firm in belief, of duty's guidance sure,
Had battled with more manfully.   At least
I am not called to answer for my fate ;
Such as it is, it must be.   It is strange
How I am changed by it ; for now the life
I longed to give up, with its every joy
Untasted, yet in possibility—
Now that its privilege is barred from me,
Now that its pains and sufferings alone
Are open to me—now I turn to it
And eager meet my portion of contempt.
I live, I live ! to struggle with my woes,
To silence conscience ; to acquit myself

Unto the world of all my debts of scorn,
To render to society its dues
Of wrong and prejudice ; to bear, uncowed,
The taunts of cowards and the threats of fools ;
To tread the same earth with the unimpeached,
Bearing myself with equal carriage firm ;
To endure the wearisome monotony
Of my existence upon sufferance ;
To hold my peace with my own frantic heart ;
Silently, constantly, to acquiesce
In my soul-degradation ; to wear on
Day after day, outwardly all engrossed
With the world's trivialities (enough
To satisfy, it seems, those whom they serve,
But sickening unto me, who must observe
Their details, lest omission should impute
Their slight of me—not my disdain of them) ;
To be yet inwardly intent absorbed
In my self-torturing consciousness of grief,
Which men without can touch not, come not near.—
This is the life that triumphs in me now ;
'Tis this impels my soul, denies it rest,
Fills it with exultation,—yea, sometimes
I have a kind of substitute for joy,
('Tis not joy's self—I have known that ; if not,
I could not know the ruin it entails :)
My sorrow has itself at last grown dear ;
I look on it with reverence, apart
From acts of folly whereto it is bound,
Apart from brief inflictions of remorse,
Associated with the unshriven sins
Whereof that sorrow is the consequent :

It hath to me an innate sacredness
That separates it from its outward signs,
Exalting it to holiness of its own.
It even seems that in comparison
Unto this sacredness—the joys of men,
Their common gladness, their deserved success,
Are yet prerogatives inadequate ;
They pall at the sublimity of mine.—
I know not whence it is, but it would seem,
That in that bliss which I unlawfully
Made seizure of—that precious, stolen joy,
No less beloved, now lost, although its loss
Be the very punishment awarded me
For my impiety—in that lost joy
There was a holiness essential
So potent, that it could not be profaned
Even by my lawless touch ; and when the joy
For evermore beyond my glimpse was drawn
Lest I, unfit for its recipience,
Should with my yearning love pollute its fame—
That holiness untainted still did cling
Unto its memory—spite of saddest shame,
Spite of the annulment of my title bold
To win and hold the glory of that dear joy :
No retribution e'er can take from me
All that the joy left with me, when 'twas gone.
My pain could not be what it is—*my* pain,
Just mine, if it were modified not so
By following upon just such bliss as mine.
The desecration has not all undone
The consecration ; somewhat of the breath
From that divine spell lingering halloweth me

In my humiliation ; and I feel
As though the very bitterness of shame—
The punishment, the penitence, the grief
That shut me in, apart from all mankind,
Were but the outer wall, that roughly guards
As in a stronghold most impregnable
The inmost sanctity of my frail bliss.
Nay, sometimes it would seem, in some rapt hour
Of inspiration, when my soul bursts free
From the pressure of the bonds that cannot quite
Paralyse all resistance—looking back
On the visioned mingling of my fatal joy
And all its after pangs of sin and grief,
That after all I did not pay too dear ;
That heaven and earth, combining to exact
Full compensation for the cheated bliss,
Though they might more inflict than all demands
Of the most vengeful justice for the offence—
Could never overdraw the payment so
As to redeem the worth of that past joy.
O ! heavenly strange is that inherent power
Of blessed memory to purify
Whatever to its sacred guardianship
Hath been entrusted ; from all vile alloy,
All dross, it separates the thing beloved,
Preserving crystal-clear its saving charm,
Keeping the best of all the soul has lost
In its apotheosis.   By this grace
There comes at times to even the worst of men,
The most defiled, the unredeemable,
Between the tossings of his troubled sleep,
In the vague hovering of his partial sense

'Twixt the dull torpor and the restless start
Of his delirious, self-destructive thought—
A momentary, vision-vivid flash
Of pure remembrance ; and he seems to see
The pictures hanging on his nursery walls,
Or the clear outline of the ancient chair,
Wherein his old nurse rocked him, long years gone ;
Nay, even the details of some transient scene
Of play-hour ; the perspective of the view
Seen at the angle of one favourite pane
In the old high-barred window, through the gap
In the branches of the tree against the wall ;
The arrangement in some corner of the toys
Strewn in profusion—order undesigned ;
Or for one moment he perceives a scent
That seems to blow across the field of hay ;
Or almost feels the soft caressing touch
Of the daisy-balls that used to pass his cheek
When other child hands flung them to and fro,
In mutual sport with him ; and the deep shower
Of dewy grass which fell against his face
As close he laid it in the clover low.
Or yet again, upon his ear there springs
With sudden sharpness, through all distance borne,
The tearing of the ivy, at the leap
Of feet whose clinging daringly let go
From the projecting stone, so good to climb ;
And the soft dry rustle of the fallen leaves
Pressed in the hurried chase 'neath tangled boughs.
Or yet, with eager, panting breath, again
Himseems that he inhales the fragrant smoke
Of the dead leaves burning in the damp, dusk air

To close with stately rite an autumn day;
Or pierces with bright youthful eyes the mist
To see the flickering gleam of the inside fire
Throw forth its waiting welcome o'er the shade
Of the winding walk, which the returning feet
After far rambles, dragged up wearily
To reach the steps between the steep, grassed banks
To the foot of the open door, proclaiming " Home ! "
Watches long seconds from the balcony
With gleeful expectation, as on morns
Of early frost, or sudden chill, to see
First sign of snowflakes shivering through the sky ;
And then calls back the flutter of joyousness
At the glad, scarce-believed discovery
Of the fine prints on the drifts of thick-massed snow,
Of bird-feet 'neath the slily scattered crumbs.
All these impressions of familiar things
Of days far past—idly, unconsciously,
Had sealed themselves upon the changing heart,
And grown into its growth, and lived its life,
Without obscuring the divinity
Of their first likeness.   These are yet his own ;
Forsake him not, as do good men, and good
Resolves at last, good hopes, and good desires ;
He may retain them in their purity,
Even to the scaffold's foot ; in the dark cell
His dreams are visited by their blest smiles ;
They fade not even before the dark of death !
So I, in the desolation of my curse,
Have visitations from the spirit pure
Of what the world deems my accursed joy—
And boast, I have not paid for it too dear !

No true joy, though it but one moment dure,
Is bought too dear, if bought with lifelong pain ;
For, through that pain, there thrills for evermore,
Subtly diffused, the essence of the joy—
Which is, indeed, itself imperishable,
And incorruptible ; it waneth not
For all the ills by which it lieth hid ;
It doth become the very spring of life—
Strength of its purpose, secret of its power,
The clue that threadeth all its mystery . . . .
While they who have their present good, laugh cold
At this sweet trust, which they illusion deem,
And mocking say—What ! you, bereft of peace,
You who have lost the right which virtue gives
Her faithful sons, to have and to enjoy,
To take their share in this world's blessings—you
Nourish yourselves with such poor travesties
Of hopes and of consolements ; you are fain
To mock yourselves with dreams—to live on dreams.
What are they good to you? They are but dreams . .
Ay ! but *good dreams* are better, better far
(And how much dearer, only dreamers know)
Than those most tangible verities, which they
Who grasp and hold them, to themselves call real,
And with much anxious care must strive to keep,
And from decay preserve ; and then, too oft
At last they lose them.   But those true delights
Which never we dare touch with hands profane,
To drag down from their holy pedestal
In the ideal fane, where dwells secure
The imperturbable image of those truths
To spirit-perception real and actual—

These are *eternal;* these alone *our own;*
These are our own, because *not only* ours,
But accessible to each member true
Of the universal brotherhood.   Our own
And one another's; mutual is the joy
With which we realise them; and that joy
Can only in its full intensity
Be felt, imparted in community.
Ah! joy sublime, too beautiful, too dear
To be delivered to the sacrilege
Of competition with the rival joys
Which to the satisfied yield happiness.
Alas! too fragile, too ethereal
To bear confrontal with the shocks of care;
It cannot lead me peacefully through life,
May not defend me from my enemies;
I cannot throw me back on its support
Against the passionate storms that surge o'er me
And shake my soul: in such dread hours, for me
It hath no promise, no comfort, and no help.
It merely is the blessing of my grief,
The sorrow that doth sanctify my sin.
But sin, and grief, and blessedness of pain,
All blend to make my life one ecstasy
Of passive tremor; of hopeless, joyless bliss.

FATE AND CREED.

Thou soul, cast down and shaken with distress—
Thou refugee, all trembling and perplexed

From the upheaval of the old beliefs
Whereto the dearest treasures of thy heart
Had been confided—Lonely, wretched one,
Comfortless in thy desolation, hear
A blessed word of sweet consolement true.
Receive a new religion ; turn thee to
Its centre, with a worship full of awe
As that which thou wouldst bring unto a God.
Take on thy lips and in thy heart its creed :—
It is but the reversal of those words
Which, at thy abjuration of all trust
In heavenly pity, and government divine,
Thou hast adopted for thy cry, to express
Thy sheer despair. " It *must be*, for *it is*."
No, no ! Let go that awful negative ;—
Search farther : see if yet thou mayst not bring
The straggling fragments of thy scattered thought
Into accordance with the master-spell
Of harmony, in these calm words pronounced—
" *It is*, because it *must be*." Think but so :
All is explained ; thus, all is rendered clear . . . .
Thou must resign thyself—for, *Fate* is *God*.

Listen, and hear Fate's message to thy soul.
"Thou hast yet my mission to achieve. Say not :—
Life will not have me, nor death : what can I do ?
What am I ? Sport of both, my own soul's curse :—
Ignorant art thou as helpless, thus to rave,
Presumptuous as despairing. Life and death
Make of thee what thou art : yet not their tool
Art thou, their victim merely ; *they* are mine ;
They mould thee to *my* purpose ; I through them

Work ; and my work is manifest, behold,
In the whole story of Humanity.
Thou, with thy deeds, thy sufferings, aud thy thoughts,
Art but an atom infinitesimal
In the great work, ever developing,
Ever progressing, 'neath my watchful eyes.
Yet thou, such as thou art, and meaner things—
The meanest, and the wretchedest, are part
Of this my work.   So art thou dignified,
So are thy pains, thy wonderings, justified !
O mortal !   Take what I accord to thee :
Fate's gifts are precious ; often when they seem
Most cruel, they possess a value rare,
Incalculable : spurn them not.—Beware
How thou dost misinterpret thy own lot—
Inviolably holy, and most high
In that it is appointed thee by *me*—
By me, to whom its desecration, oft
Threatened by thy unreasoning, impious scorn,
Were insult deadly, treason blasphemous.
Thou, who bewailest with such wild lament
The sufferings of thy life—what knowest thou
Of my sublimest purpose, whereunto
I deign to make them instrument ?   Thy wrongs,
Thy errors irretrievable—for them
Why dost thou soil thy soul with vain regrets ?
How darest thou, incapable !—to judge
Of the ingredients which I cast into
The great alembic, whence I would distil
Eternal types ?—Futurity is mine,
My preparation from the *present* of thee,
And of thy human fellows ; and what share

Therein shall fall to thee—that is alone
Worthy thy aspiration or desire :
And so much only as there shall endure
From toils and pains, from efforts and from strifes,
From enterprise of mortals—of all this
So much as shall abide in its results
To mould one other single destiny,
To modify one circumstance, to bend
The standard of one recognised ideal—
To impress a during stamp on flexile Time—
So much, no more, is counted to the score
Of each one's life.   So, if Posterity
Upon thy weakness buildeth strength, then I
Have in that strength the satisfaction full
Of finished purpose ; and in mine, be thine.
In my achievement find thy only bliss,
Though it absorb not only thy dear life,
But the whole energies, and the best love
Of countless thousands, struggling like to thee
Through age on age ; each being but a step
Up to the consummation I design,
Wherein each aspirant shall reach his crown,
Each individual life having its part
In the one general ultimate victory
For the human struggle.—O, ye striving ones,
Look backward, on the lives of all the past,
And make comparison.   The happy ones
That calm have glided to a peaceful end,
Merged in the common joys which were their goal,
Enough unto themselves, having of toil
Reward, for effort duly recompense,
And self-exhausting satisfaction felt

In every moment separate and complete
Of their existence finished. . . Well. Such lives—
What impress have they made? What more is left
When they are done? What rules, what thoughts,
   what acts
Salute them ancestors? . . . They are effaced,
And with them all the capabilities
That lay in them, of which ye nought may know.
But those which stand out darkly from the page
Of history (which men this world's record deem)
Authentic, or of story (which, indeed,
Is record—though of spirits, not of names)—
The lives that stand out terribly distinct
With their appendages of curse and crime,
Of anguish wrestled with, of shame subdued,
Those whose career has isolated them
In an existence of their own, apart
From the surrounding gladness and content—
An utter loneness of unthinkable woe ;—
Whose thoughts, whose darings, and whose sufferings,
Yea, even whose brand of infamy—remain
To their descendants of mankind, to show
New combinations of the elements
Eternal, still new secrets to reveal
Of spiritual mysteries—. . . *These* have lived.
Would ye undo their actions? or recal
Their soul-throes? Wield compulsion o'er those lives,
To set them in conformity unto
The even current of the markless crowd?
They are your life, ye mortals of to-day ;
Ye learn your lessons from their pictured deeds,
Inspire your poems with their breathing pain,

Immortalise their transitory pangs ;
In following up their deviating tracks
Find clues to guide you through the labyrinth
Of the untried ; from their experiments
Induce new rules for your philosophy.
Ye see, in them, the universe condensed—
See them diffused into the universe. . . .
Choose, then, if ye *could* choose ; choose which ye
    would—
The perpetuity of mind, through strife,
In infinite essence, or the blissful state
Which, by its nature's limits, tends unto
Its own annihilation.   But 'tis vain—
Thou mayst not choose : I choose for thee : but thou,
Know, now, my choice, and see that it is good.
Take thou my revelation. . . . *I am Fate.*"

That is Fate's message.   Wilt thou not accept
The charter that she thus holds out to thee,
Initiating thee in the privilege
Of her high order ? mystic brotherhood,
Whose pass-word, that grand word *necessity*,
So holy, so sufficing to all those
Who are admitted of the fellowship,
Is yet uncomprehended, meaningless,
To the profane,—as *thou* hast been—shut out
From that most blest communion.   Ponder well
The dictates of that voice divine, whereby
Thy frantic, fearful doubts shall be allayed.
Without that revelation, what art thou ?
What hast thou left to lean on ? Ah, too well
Thou knowest thy destitution.   For how long

Thy constant prayer hath been, " Save me from life ! "
More thou hast known not how to ask ; and less
Not dared, since that one moment that revealed
In its unutterable horror to thee
Thy powerlessness to strive against thy doom.
And ever since that moment, thou hast writhed
In consciousness of degradation.   Yea,
The cry wrung from thy lips in agony,
" O, take this curse away from me ! "—that cry
That was not answered—echoes in thy heart
With an eternal mockery.   Thou deemst
It was not heard ?   Ah ! call that moment back,
If thou *canst* clearly bring it back to thought
Dissociated from its madness.—Yea,
The curse which thou hadst borne so long, the curse
Laid upon thee by Fate, the curse of *life*—
Thou didst cry out, at last, in rage, and say
It was too hard—too horrible to bear !
God would not answer thee—Chance did not send
Relief; thyself wouldst judge thy righteous cause,
Wouldst brave the end.   .   .   .   .   .
.   .   .   .   What was it held thee back ?—
Thy good or evil genius ? . . . In thy soul
Wild fury raved o'er its own impotence ;
All was undone—thy utmost effort failed ;
The way was barred by which thou wouldst escape
The ills which crowded in conspiracy
For thy destruction : thou wert self-deceived ;
Thy trusted refuge had but proved a snare
To drag thee farther into the full swing
Of forces on thy ruin concentrate.
There was no freedom from their baleful strength

To be by most stupendous effort won ;—
The extreme step, upon whose boasted power
Thy contemplation long had stayed itself
For the assertion of thy bold intent
Was tried—and failed thee.   In the supreme test
Thy will was dulled, thy triumph snatched away,
Thy struggling hope crushed down for evermore,
Thy soul confounded—thy resistance cowed. . .
So, in thy passionate self-reproach, thy storm
Of loathing and humiliation—thus
Didst thou, defiant, utter impiously
The challenge to the demon of thyself,
Accursing.—" On my own head be the blood
Of all the future sorrow, sin and shame,
For me and mine, that may accrue from this—
This act of indecision ; this retreat
From my fixed purpose ; this failure of my will
To execute its own long-formed decree,
To give effect at last to its resolve
Well reasoned out, and utterly.   Now I see
I must be henceforth, as before, the prey
Of my spontaneous deeds, my unforeseen
Impulses, and the baneful influence
Of my resistless fellows—friends or foes." . . . .
Now from that frenzy which possessed thee then
Thou art recovered.   Summon all thy strength
Of mind, and on this question bring to bear
Thy judgment calm, . . . *What was it held thee back?*
What was it, but the spirit of all life,
The spirit irresistible governing
Within thee, but not of thee ; which pervades
All organisms, all individual forms

That give expression separate to the one
Force vital, thus in each pervading all ;
The spirit, undiscerned so long by thee,
That dominates all actions, and that rules
In every interruption,—every pause
Of energy,—in every seeming waste
As well as in success ; that vindicates
Every expenditure by final aim ;
That harmonises impulse and event,
Adapting most conflicting influences
Unto the absolute certainty—their end. . . .
Learn thou but this. Assimilate thy will
Unto this fatalism that swayeth it.
Seek not to guide the forces infinite
With which thou art confront, with which to cope
Thy partial knowledge must be, can but be
Inadequate. Cease the perplexing toil
Of wresting circumstances from their ends
To accord them with *thy* reason ; cease the attempt
To avert those consequences that depend
Upon a power not thine—which to construe
Is to thy might all as impossible
As to possess it, or to look into
Its origin. Cease to oppose to Fate
Thy erring will, thy vacillating thought, ·
Thy labour of endeavour ; it must be
Without avail—believe it, ere too late.
Hast thou not seen, what the result hath been
Of thy impassioned efforts ?—Thy resolve
(And thou wast resolute, with all the strength
Of instinct) in confusion had its end.
The voice that spoke within thee, urging thee

To meditation of the desperate act
Which some inscrutable, inconceivable power
Has thwarted. . . . . Seemed it not to rule in thee
With so imperious an authority
That thou must cherish such a faith in it
As others feel in laws they deem divine ? . . .
Thou wouldst obey it, as thy being's law :
But it is overmastered. How ? By what ? . . .
The terrible mystery hath flung thy soul
Into its lowest depths of agony.
Thy terror has unmanned thee. Now look up—
All is not over. Thou mayst yet be brave
If thou wilt look thy destiny in the face,
Dare it, but not defy it. Thou must drink
Yet deeper of the cup of suffering,
It is not all exhausted : there must be
More sorrow yet, more wrong reserved for thee.
Thou by endurance canst aloue fulfil
Thy duty, and redeem thy spirit's pledge
To the invisible powers of life. That pledge
Were forfeit, shouldst thou keep the awful vow
Which thou hast perjured. Yet, now, think thee well ;
Remember, how thou wouldst have kept it ; how
Thou hast raved, because thou couldst not keep it. Say,
Was not thy prayer heard ? Came the answer not
In that divine refusal, which did blight,
O fool ! thy futile and imperfect scheme
With its negation ? Nay, God heard thy prayer ;
The Fate-god gave thee succour in that hour
Of mortal danger ;—saved thee from *thyself.* . . .
Prayer ! Answer ! Is Fate dallied with by prayers ?
Doth the eternal reason fluctuate

For human protestation or appeal ?—
Nay, rather, the immovable decree
Was with thy groan of prayer compatible ;
That prayer but showed the converse to its seal,
The correspondence in thy spirit's law
With the universal order, whereunto
It is subincident, subordinate . . .
Now, brace thy faculties, in readiness
For their predestined function ; be thou true
To thy election ; waver, hence, no more
In thy sworn service to thy God, to Fate.
There may be crime ordained thee to commit :—
So, then, with holy, desperate resolve
Commit that crime ; and it shall find its place
In the full cycle of the ordinance
Of Destiny.   Still hold to thy firm faith
In thy new God, necessity, which takes
The place, to thee, of thy abandoned *Law;*
Tremble not at the apparent negligence
Of the new order, which disorder seems
To thee, whose point of view long time hath been
In error ; and so in changing suddenly,
Thy sight at first is dazzled and confused ;
All seems involved in inconsistency ;
Thou canst not find the beauty of symmetry
Which thou hast sought, whose absence thou hast
      mourned
In thy vain search through shattered systems false
Whose wrecks crowd on thy orbit, and impede
Thy vision of the horizon clear beyond.—
Tremble not, doubt not ; keep thy thoughts still free,
And thy will pure ; still think thou holily,

And, through whatever actions intricate
The force of life bear thee, resisting, on—
Thou shalt have Fate's support; her strengthening
    word
To nerve thee for the conflict; in thy need
Communion sanctifying ; in thy shame
Her sweetest consolation ; for thy sin
Her *absolution.* Henceforth, be thy prayer
Not "Let this cup pass from me :" but, as He
Whose suffering ignominy for so long
Hath glorified mankind, to *his* God cried—
" Not my will, *thine* be done." . . . It *shall* be *done :*
The one will only is omnipotent :
And, conscious or unconscious, all the laws
By which men frame their conduct, or by which
The conduct of the inanimate universe
Is governed—all from *this* will are derived.
The issues of all struggles must conform,
The ends of all diversity in means
Must be adapted to—Necessity.

NOT KNOWING.

(From a passage in a biography.)

" He died, not knowing."   And Fame's laurels swung
  Their garlands pendant o'er his after name.
He thought that vainly he had wept and sung ;—
  O sad ! to die without the grasp of Fame.

Fame !—to have reached to her the striving hands,
  To have languished for one far glimpse of her smile,
Only to be repulsed—the bold demands
  With shame requited, turned to mockery vile.

To have set life's fairest, dearest gifts at nought,
  Flouted her injuries with calm disdain,
For the hot pursuit of one absorbing thought,
  The intensity whose thrill could numb all pain ;

To have travailed, in the loneliness and dread
  Of that deep life, forsaken by repose,
With revelation of innate truths unsaid,
  And brought it forth with sharp exceeding throes ;

Through all existence to have felt the strain
  Of powers to which full utterance was denied,
To have sought their knowledge true with yearnings
    vain,
  —O cruel ! and not knowing, to have died !

The consciousness within himself to bear
   Of sacred gifts, committed to his charge,
Yet recognised not : the long, sick despair
   Of the failing mission, with its scope so large :

Forced by the expansion of world-stretching thought,
   Impelled by the hidden working of pent rage
To cry with irrepressible cry, that sought
   To cry out ringing to the coming age—

That sought to echo age on age beyond,
   O'er all the sympathetic clangs of earth,
To sound through many a cry responsive fond
   —And self to have deemed it stifled at its birth !

To feel towards all the human brotherhood
   In the simultaneous pulse of their one woe
—Reflecting all their evil, all their good,
   —To feel for them—to touch—and not to know !

O ! call it not light vanity, the wild
   Untamable longing for the ecstatic state
Where only can such pangs be reconciled,
   Where only is such anguish compensate.

Mistake it not—nor trifle with its power,
   That passionate fervour, that mad love of fame . . .
What is it ?   Wish for life's success as dower ?
   Desire to be remembered by a name ?

Not that, not that for which he fearful pined,
   Whose worship ceaseless quite consumed away

All energy of will and heart and mind,
    All but the strength for that one boon to pray !

It was in him the eager, one desire
    Which none who hath would lose, spite of its pain,
That the moments which had flushed 'neath holy fire
    Should ever semblance of its glow retain.

That the sense, which once had palpitated fleet
    In answer to the tremble of touch divine,
Should not let fade the impression strange and sweet,
    Nor be extinct in one faint memory fine.

That those grand visions, which could ne'er be told,
    Should not be lost, without much struggle and strife ;
That the wondrous burden in his faltering hold
    Should whelm him not, nor sink from him with life.

That the soul-blood which he spilt on the hard plain
    Of arid life, might nourish future flowers ;
That sparks of spirit-glory from his pain
    Might shoot forth into the eternal hours.

So did he spend his life in writhings strong
    To embody but one thought that might abide :
But all the efforts, all the wonder long
    Won him not triumph.   Knowing not, he died.

Lives, in their vast shoals sweeping endless on
    Are transient manifest, and pass away :
. . . They are too many to be known ; are gone
    Without a trace that may survive the day.

They give forth noisy sounds, in busy hum,
  Each undistinguished in the general jar ;
Then, after each other, with each other, dumb
  They fall :—Such are the countless lives that are.

Yet all lives live not to themselves ; beyond
  They call, to one another, and are heard :
They pass—yet where be souls that can respond
  They linger in the lives that they have stirred.

But even thus, their impress swift is past ;
  The blended sounds, the nutual lives, must die ; . . .
Yet there are universal lives, that last
  From life to life, keeping identity—

Lives that are part of every life that strives;
  Whose thoughts have share in every human lot ;
Whose voice, not hushed, quivers through sounding
    lives—
  And his was one, although he knew it not.

He knew not ; but it was so.   Not for him
  The satisfaction, but for us, to know ;
We, by analogy, interpret dim
  The reason whose secret can console our woe. . . .

To live, not knowing !—O hard doom, which we
  Must yield to !—That dear bliss that might have
    been,
We have been cheated of ; but if it be
  By falseness or by fate, we may not ween.

O, not to know !—to have the dull regret
   That aches in many a life, through all its moan
Never explained, never redeemed. . . . Ah ! yet,
   It may be. . . What *we* know not *shall be known.*

"AFLOAT." (SCHWÄRMEREI).

FAMILIAR Spirit ! Unto thee
How long have I been devote, my sea !
To thee am I pledged by solemn vow,
Often and often renewed :—and now
It seems as though thou didst call to me
"Remember thy fealty to the sea !"

I have sworn, my first love shall be my last ;—
If I have been fickle in times long past—
If my fancy hath fluttered, my will oft ranged
O'er frivolous lovers ;—my heart, unchanged,
Still incorruptible unto thee
Hath guarded its loyalty, O my sea !

Light is my heart ; scarce I feel it beat,
As though thou didst rock it to slumber sweet ;
On my lips yet lingers the ripple's kiss—
None other defile them, after this !—
O ! blest to die in a wave's embrace,—
To smile, as it laughed up into my face,
With a smile that no sadness should e'er allay,
That no more in tears should fade away—
The old, old longing comes back to me
To end my life in its love—in the sea !

I lean back ;—my head is on thy breast :
Ah ! Never in human arms would I rest ;
They could not be tender and strong as thine,
To bear me up as I calm recline,
In a rapturous sense that pervades me all :—
Thou tirest not—never wilt let me fall—
Yet thou holdest me not as in bonds ; no need
To shrink from thy touch, lest its power impede
My force of will ;—I resist not thee ;
I struggle not ; for thou leavest me free ;—
Free, though so closely unto thee pressed—
I feel not thy grasp ; my will is at rest.
Without restraint, I may listless glide—
I may toss my arms, I may fling them wide—
Thou vauntest no mastery over me ;—
And yet, thou knowest I am thine, my sea !

Yes—thine ! I am thine !—Wilt thou claim me now ?
Wilt thou bear me away, to redeem my vow ?
Assert thy lordship ! Unto thy sway
My heart is responsive, and must obey :
Keep me more close—do not let me go ;—
I know thy language : speak to me low
In the mystic voice I have learnt to hear,
Which so oft has murmured its secrets dear
To my spirit, that understands—O, well !
Love can interpret the weirdest spell.
In darkness, and stillness, unto me
Thou hast spoken ; and I have listened to thee :
Mysterious communion hath been between
Thee and me ; for love-tokens have there been
Symbols I treasure—none else has known

Their meaniug ;—they tell me I am thine own.—
—Say to me—" Darliug ! " I will hear
And answer the summons : I do not fear
To follow thy call.—O ! let me be
With thee for ever, my sea ! my sea !

RUE.

"Six months ago, this morn, I made a vow ;—
    And broke it ere the eve!
  O ! had I been more loyal, surely now
    I had not thus to grieve.

"Let it be past—all that hath been between ;
    Here would I fain efface
From my life's record what too dear hath been,
    Even to its faintest trace.

"Upon my heart I boasted once to set,
    When it should come forth free,
A seal, in one word— *Vinci :*—And even yet
    That word its seal *shall* be.

"Let now the wild confusion be all o'er,
    That sprang from one rash hour ;
Its wilderment entangle me no more—
    I have freed me from its power.

"After the long life lived in so short a space
    My vow do I renew ;
Not quite in vain its lessons I retrace—
    This time, I will be true!"

AUF WIEDERSEHEN.

In the sacred brotherhood of universal sympathy
We were two brothers :—in the mystic bond we vowed
    to be
True to each other, far beyond all time. We chose
    to bear
A secret pledge to one another, on the heart to wear,
Sign of our holy order, that should be perpetually
Truth-talisman, and signet-seal of our love's mystery ;
We chose a watchword, which should each to each
    , henceforth betray
Whatever lapse of years, or change of scene, should
    cross our way.
We, that had looked in one another's souls so soon,
    and known
So quickly, all the mutual truths learnt by close love
    alone,
We promised that the word I gave him, should we
    meet again,
Was to be our recognition-token:—this—"*Auf Wieder-
    schen.*"

On the battle-field we parted, as we met ; new friends,
    to part ;
New friends, with all the trust of oldest friendship at
    the heart ;

Comrades, for once, in duty—severed then, at duty's
    call,
With the mystic bond uniting us, invisible through all.
And our only words at parting were the words he bade
    remain
Treasured up for future greeting—first and last—
    " Auf Wiedersehen."

.   .   .   .   .   .

Now, oft I ask myself the question, tortured with
    these new
Sad doubts, undreamed of in our early faith.—Is it
    still true,
The blest, mysterious union I believed in long ago?
Or has it lost its virtue?　Shall I let my clinging go?
My trustful clinging to its subtle potency? . . . We
    said
No fate could ever separate true soul friends, living
    or dead,
But . . . . Can our bond endure, ignoring even the
    bounds of Time?
Did our imperfect speech translate aright the truth
    sublime
That we sought with all love's daring to interpret?—
    Are there set
No limits to the claims by which our spirits, even yet,
Demand unbroken fellowship? May yet some power fulfil
The *pledge still unredeemed*—made void unto our im-
    potent will?
Do they hold good, those words whose fond remem-
    brance seems to be—
Must be, unless such unknown power there be—mere
    mockery?

We met no more.   How shall we meet ?—The blessed
    words remain
Unspoken ; in my heart the waiting watchword rests
    in vain,
Unchallenged ; and the longing thought in life un-
    satisfied
Is carried to the awful sphere beyond ; the love that
    cried
Disconsolate so oft, doth lift itself with strong desire,
And dareth of eternity importunate require
Answer to its unresting plea. . . . If in infinity
Renewal of this life, however modified, may be—
If soul force in the scope ahead shall find expression
    still ;
If, through all changing, be defined identity of will—
May the pledges here annulled be recognised, accepted,
    there ?
The struggling spirit-claims acknowledged, after their
    despair ?
And our watchword, unimpaired by its delay, full
    meaning gain
Even as earnest and fulfilment all in one ?   *Auf
    Wiedersehen !*

WAVE OMENRY.

I HAVE just seen two waves meet, face to face ;
One with the ebb was coming, one with the flow ;
Before they broke into that rash embrace
I thought each had a separate way to go ; —
Each had its own, its separate way to go—
But what of either track doth now appear ?
Have the two blent together, or still near
Kept, and so changed their current ? Who doth know

How close upon each other they two clung,
With showering kisses of impetuous spray !
Passionately their curling arms they flung
To twine each other. —So they lost their way ;
In intermingling so, they lost their way !—
But soon the opposite forces in them tore
Inevitably them asunder ;—and bore
On their first destined way, unaltered ? Nay !

The motive wherewith each had been endued
Had in the shock, which for a moment blent
Each with the other's, been of both subdued—
The mutual energy had all been spent.
Each had destroyed the other ; itself each spent ;
No force was left ; the rush, the speed were gone ;

D

After the parting, each must slow drag on
Waning and listless.—Ah ! could waves repent !

The scattered waters crawl, subside, efface—
Vain struggle !—effort vain against the innate
Tendence :—resistance fails to leave its trace ;
For waves, for man, there is one rule, one fate ;—
For waves, for man, there is one law, one fate ;
The warm heart in us may deny its sway ;
The will revolt, in protest, as it may—
And, trying its counter might—submit, too late !

Two lives may meet ; upon each one impressed
Purport distinct, direction of its own ;
And for brief space of love's deluding rest
They merge into each other, and seem as one ;—
Would thwart their different destiny and be one,
Guide their course, form a path :—But hence must go,
Parted, and scattered ;—broken powers, to flow
In the wide waste of being, lost, unknown !

VERITAS VICTRIX.

A VOICE spoke, long ago, within my soul,
Waking it urgently, with sudden start,
To consciousness of revelation :—" Truth
Is mighty, and must prevail."—And then I took
Those fatal words to be my talisman,
To fix the aims of all my coming life,
Absorb its interests, guide its vague career,
And fill its one devotion. . . . . For I thought
That that same voice in the eternal years
Should speak to me once more, and thrill through me
For but one moment, which should henceforth live
In my whole being for ever. . . . . .

                        But I learnt
My motto wrongly, in my rash, fond pride ;
And ever, rushing through the chaos of thoughts
And things and phantasms round me, at wild speed
On my own way, I gloried to myself,
Saying, " Truth indeed is mighty ; and *by that
I will prevail!*" . . . . I could not fail !—In spite
Of the opposition, the perversity
Of facts and speculations, that the more
I struggled with them, seemed the less to yield,
My trust in my almighty talisman
Kept constant my defiance : and I said—
" I *must* be Victor." . . . .

On my soul, at last,
Fell fearful certainty, that broke the spell
Of my most dear delusion.—Shudderingly
Feeling that I was mocked, I cried, " O Truth !
How have I been deceived !   My hopes in thee
How cruelly betrayed !—Disdainful Truth,
I am not thy soldier, but thy conscript, then—
Thy victim, not thy martyr !   I may die
For thee, or live without thee ; but to thee
'Tis all the same ; thou smilest still serene,
Turning thy cold face from me ; thou dost pass
O'er ages, o'er the universe, in march
Triumphal, and dost tread beneath thy feet
Thy votaries ;—and the passionate souls that bound,
With aspirations, to obstruct thy way,
Falling before thy path, to worship thee
And have their homage once accepted of thee,
Are swept aside at thy approach, to make
Free passage for thee ; and thou, haughtily,
Gliding on even course, dost leave them prone
With prayers unheeded, grovelling in despair,
No longer subjects—suppliants nevermore,
With hope to serve thee, and with wish to rise
And play the hero for thee—but thy *slaves*,
Crushed and confounded, baffled, scorned, and quelled !
—But I shall never see thee.   Go thy way,
And I will go in my own might, nor strive
To look upon thee ; but sustain the fight
Into whose press I am flung, unhelped by thee ;
Nor seek to give thee glory, nor to win
Thy blessing—since my cause no more is thine ! "

So, I went on my way; and wearily
Wrestled with powers of darkness and of dread,
With shapes of horror undefined, with might
Indomitable; met them, one by one,
Desperate and all unaided. But although
I had no hope, no aim, no meaning even
To animate me—still, with firm resolve,
With dull, unflinching effort, did I keep
The obligations of the conflict; still
I wavered not, nor turned aside, whate'er
Danger or terror on my forward path
Threatened my progress.—I went on; and stopped
Before each strange encounter on my way,
To question it; and would not be denied,
Demanding satisfaction absolute
To my continuous challenge;—though no end
To my endurance could I faint descry,
I yielded not, but wrestled; would not tire
Though weary, weary. . . .
                                        And it then befel
To me, as unto Jacob, when 'tis told
His adversary did become his God
After his awful wrestling. Unto me
One came, and wrestled with me. . . . I had said
"I will be victor," in my boastful pride,
And—I *was vanquished*: . . . But my victor was God!
For it was Truth, at last, on whom I had looked
Unwitting face to face—the unknown God!
And, when the struggle was over—only then
I knew by what sublime and heavenly power
I had been overcome; and found with joy
That the past struggle left a blessing with me;—

Yea, that that might that had subdued my own
Was henceforth *mine ;* from my resistance vain
The strength I could not baffle, was become
My guerdon, and the prize of victory,
More dear than victory self.   And from that time
No longer has my watchword been, for self
" Victor ! "—But now with sacred awe I guard
This watchword, which upon my heart I bear—
" *Veritas* Victrix ! " . . . Thus doth truth prevail !

Veritas Viotrix ! . . . That was the true voice. . . .
And surely. . . . I shall hear it speak—again !

THE LAST LOOK.

I. DESPONDENCY.

AND is it death?   The dear, the lovely form
   Lies, O so restful ! where 'twas wont to rest :
So softly, so serenely, I would fancy
   In slumber sweet those eyelids still were prest.

Herself we loved : yet we could only know
   Her spirit bodied in its earthly home ;
This was the only token we might cherish
   For her : her soul breathed to us *hence* alone.

We could not the pure spirit, then, behold—
   That was too holy for these mortal eyes
To gaze upon ; the soul all fair, unclothéd
   Hath being that we cannot realise.

But its dear dwelling was this silent form
   From which we watched it, awfully, depart ;
Dissolv'd is that mysterious, subtle union—
   Cold are the lips, and motionless the heart.

This solemn presence, that we feel so near,
   Dispels the tender thoughts that wont to rest
So fondly on our dear one's loved image,
   And ruthless breaks the ties once sweet and blest.

Bowed down beneath the dark and dreadful spell
　　Our souls yield yearningly, with futile strife,
All the long hallowed, old associations
　　That cling around our darling's silenced life.

Now, thought is baffled in the trembling search
　　To track her spirit in those regions wide
So far removed from our faint contemplation. . . .
　　But yesterday, she was so near our side—

Close by us ! face to face !　And as we gazed
　　We saw *her* smile on us :—she was *our own.* . . .
Now, parted from us—by what dread transition ?
　　What is she ?—Inconceivable ! unknown !

So like to us, a little while ago—
　　Nay, one of us . . . . how strange to think upon !
—Lost unto us—merged in the great Eternal—
　　Beyond our failing love for ever gone !

. . . . To look into the mysteries of death,
　　How fearful ! from our partial view, this side—
And she—alone—hath entered, past recalling,
　　The infinite, wildering depths, all dark, untried !

No word for us from these lips more shall fall ;—
　　And all the long communion that hath been,
Is *that* no more ?　So quick sunk in oblivion
　　For her and us, with death's veil drawn between ?

These gentle hands so often we have pressed,
　　The dear, bright eyes whose gaze we loved to meet—

No more give sign to us ; nor love nor pity,
 Nor trust, respondeth to our love so sweet.

We cannot near her in the wildest dream ;
 We may not stretch our hands forth, tremblingly,
To feel one last, fond, clinging grasp : unspoken
 Love's wistful message in the heart must lie.

Those passionate *last words—too late* were said . . . .
 We send them after, through the dark, in vain ! . .
Our anxious thoughts—we know not if they follow,
 Nor if her own look back to us again !

O, cruel parting !—Souls that here so true
 Through life have kept together, side by side,
Must thus all fearfully be rent asunder,
 And mourning hearts be left unsatisfied !

No possible, that this great mystery
 Be solv'd ; but only the stern certainty
That the inevitable, though it tarry
 Cometh—and we must bear it, helplessly.

And so we say—Farewell.　O Destiny
 Inscrutable !　How pitiless is Fate !
It *must* be :—for, it *is*.　Farewell, farewell, farewell, O
  dearest ! . . . .
 Thought droops, when it would soar to reach thy
  state !

II. INTUITION.

Bend we down tenderly, to gaze once more
   On the dear face, still features, closéd eyes
Which still retain the semblance of our loved one
   In their long rest, where still such beauty lies.

We may not call her ours again, on earth ;
   We may not see the beauteous face again ;
Our last fond look of it must now be taken—
   It hath no smile more now, to soothe our pain.

. . . Then must we sever all our thoughts of her
   From the familiar face o'er which we weep ?
How can we bring her back into our fancy ?
   What image of her now can memory keep ?

. . . Ah ! she is *far away* : her spirit fair
   Hath found the endless path, that opens bright
Beyond these gloom-closed realms, wherefrom—mist-
      hidden—
   We seek in vain the all-revealing light.

Herself still lives ; the full and perfect life
   Of which our shrinking minds no form can frame.
Hope, dreaming, flies on dim, mysterious traces,
   And—in far glimpses—*sees her*—still the same !

Interprets all the inspirations fleet
   Which holy love breathes into our frail thought,
And trusts to Truth to show, at its unfolding,
   All realised that we have daring sought.

She is not changed—unless the sweet hope err,
    And our high longings have aspired in vain—
But the blest spirit, freed from fleshly fetters,
    Unto its native freedom doth attain.

We have not known that spirit as it is ;
    Earth's ties have bound it down, birth quelled its
        powers,
Stain'd its pure essence, marred its heavenly likeness,
    Made it *seem* mortal—like these souls of ours.

But yet, believe, nought can that force subdue
    Which, proudly conscious, struggles through our life
To assert itself o'er doubt, despair, and blindness,
    And gains, at last, the mastery in the strife.

At last !—yes ; this grand principle of life
    Shall break forth, following Hope's triumphant
        flight,
From th' intricate path that windeth through our
        darkness
    —And, sudden, burst upon the heaven-beamed light.

And in that rapture, kindred souls shall meet
    And learn to know each other, as ne'er before ;
Take up familiar converse, long years broken,
    To endure, thenceforth, tireless, for evermore.

Then will our darling look on us again,
    And we behold *her*—shining in clearest light. . . . .
Till then, she still shall linger in our memory.
    In this dear form on which we gaze to-night !

THE MEANING.

Man, fretful murmuring o'er his lot—proud man,
    reviling Fate,
Complains of unrequited griefs, of pains inadequate ;
Moans o'er the sorrow without end, the anguish borne
    in vain,
That mock his insufficient life with its unmeaning pain.
Nor aught avails the eager strife of even the bravest
    mind
In its impassioned effort yet some hidden law to find,
Some universal law, whose revelation shall contain
Both *purpose* of the mystery, and interpretation plain :—
That may not be ; man must not hope unto his
    destiny
For reason it will render him e'er reconciled to be :
We may not grapple with the cause of life's bewilder-
    ment,
Nor harmonise perplexities, whilst we are still intent
On finding some solution that shall answer for *our* weal ;
On recognising as divine guidance that *we* can feel.—
Alas ! the futile task !—Even hope it passes, as belief :
Not unto us the satisfaction we demand of grief ;
Not for *our* sake our sufferings :—it seems we have no
    claim
To read ourselves the charm writ in our lives, or spell
    its name.

But in our groping dreams, a faint conjecture dim doth
    sway
Sometimes ; it hovers o'er the soul, and points out, far
    away
Mysterious looming in deep shade, a possibility
Full of promise, wherein folded may the glorious
    meaning lie.

May it not be that, far beyond the range of human
    soul
Infinite spirits have their scope ? And unto their control
Be ordered every detail of the universe, that we
See but imperfectly, we beings of a low degree,
Conceiving false relations of the inconceivable whole,
Deeming ourselves the acme —knowing not the higher
    soul,
Whose motions to our consciousness can be no more
    made clear
Than our thoughts can be translated to a firefly :
    —Were not here
A glimpse of the analogy that may establish reign
Between us and the exalted ones to whom the *rest* is
    plain ?—
Does not the world, as known to us, with forms of
    being throng
All far removed from our high state ? And do not all
    belong
To us ?—and to our spirits do not all, however far
In grade from one another severed, seem but what they
    are
For *our* interpretation? That we read them, as we
    will,

And behold their pains and glory, for our explanation
    still?

Some little joys they find to make their own life glad
    and bright;

The butterfly's existence may be gay with brief delight;

The bird that warbles in our bowers tunes not unto
    our ear

His joyous song; yet it *is* ours, the song so blissful
    clear,

Albeit outpouring from the fulness of a heart, whose
    strain

Bursts forth as from a child's heart laughs forgetful-
    ness of pain.

And the songless birds, that twitter through their day
    unsought, unknown,

May find their life entire one spell of blessedness
    their own—

Yet they—for us—exist not; when they die, they have
    not been. . . .

And loveliness and gladness seem in soulless things
    oft seen—

But only for the joy they render, only unto earth

The adornment of their beauty, do we count their lives
    of worth.

And equally do we deem blessed whatever for our joy

We torture, or despoil; what for our service we
    destroy.

The bee, that toils so peacefully among the summer
    flowers—

How beautiful and fit we find her work; . . . for it is ours;

The purpose of her busy life, the end of all her toil,

Submits itself to our luxurious wish, becomes our spoil.

The lovely things with plumage for whose sake they
    must be slain ;

The powerful ones whose strength, the weak whose
    frailty is our gain ;

The forms of life ephemeral whose gifts but glad our
    eye ;

The toilers who bequeath their beauteous work to us,
    then die ;

The storers of our priceless pearls, our treasures from
    the scas,

Corals of wondrous beauty, perfect shell-shapes. . . .
    What are these

But creatures that in countless shoals are crowded,
    life on life,

Merely that the results of labour whence their lives
    were rife

Should yield such pleasure for our ease ?—How many,
    then, again,

Are formed but for the pleasure that is yielded from
    their pain ?

Whose fluttering agony may for awhile subserve our
    taste—

Ours are they ; ours to wound, to bruise, to maim, to
    kill, to waste—

For the luxury of splendid hues, rich dyes, or fair
    threads fine,

For the momentary gleams of tints in dying throes
    that shine—

All use, all combinations that have been since Time
    began,

Of animate and inanimate things—are for the use of
    man.

And if the helpless things could choose whether or not
    to be

(Were they endowed with reason for the choice, to
    judge as we)

If they could but discern what were the functions,
    which to fill

Was their existence called for,—minister to human
    will—

Would they grudge to us the gladness from their life
    derived ? or say

That their beauty, useless unto them, as well were
    thrown away ?

That their pains, from which the source of man's de-
    light must be supplied

Were purposeless ?   That that brief space of time
    before they died

Was the measure of their meaning ? that the world's
    plan were the same

Whether or not their transitory phantasms went and
    came ?

—They might : but we, unmoved, should still regard
    them as our own,

Still see the need which they were formed to satisfy
    alone,

Still feel that it was just to look on them as made to
    be

Material for our art to work upon ; no cruelty

In using them to gratify delight of sense or mind

Should we reproach to us.   Should we not vindication
    find

In the law of compensation ?—fitness thus of means
    to end ?

And find all purposes fulfilled that well with ours
would blend?
See the comprehension of the lower in the higher life,
Whose perfecting subordinates all agents, without
strife?

.   .   .   .

So we, whose pains of life seem all arranged so
carelessly,
We may be good to play with—to be played by
Destiny.
From our struggles agonising, may there not evolved be
(Well may we dare to guess it : be it not so, how
know we ?—)
Some joyous apparition, some sublime, transcendent
sight,
Which to faculties we reck not of may bring intense
delight ?
Unknown of us, there may exist some powers of being,
higher
Than our dull consciousness can reach, our tremulous
desire ;
The mysteries of such life must from our wistful gaze
e'er be
Hidden ; or but with partial sense, and awe confused,
may we
Behold in some surpassing sign of nature manifest
One trait of the manifold might, the wondrous energies, that rest
In the spirits unrevealed—which are for us to grasp
or know
What we are to the creeping things on which our eyes
may glow.

E

If we could think that blessed eyes which we shall
    never see
Saw transient gleams of beauty flash from our brief
    agony;
Could we think that webs were woven whose bright
    hues we ne'er may know,
From threads that we unceasing spin out from our
    lives of woe—
That all our failing purposes were, by a perfect art,
Worked into a beauteous plan in whose delight we
    have no part;
That our dear, imperfect schemes, broken off in their
    deficiency,
Were for higher ends adapted to heavenly symmetry;
That some fine sense, inconceivable by ours, could
    ours conceive,
Could in quiverings of Time eternal harmony perceive,
Might we not, satisfied, our self-hood and its love
    resign,
Acknowledging that infinite sense that felt by us,
    divine?. . . .
Were it not well to look upon our passions as the
    thrill
To which that sense beyond us should respond? Yea,
    might not still
Our human faint endeavour, that had failed to com-
    prehend
That unknown being into whose reality we blend.
Call it *God?* And with mute worship to its spell our
    spirits bow,
And live *in it*, as we live *for it*—die once, and suffer
    now?—

THE OUTCAST AND THE CHILD.

"Do I love thee?" . . . .   Only from a little child
Could such a question e'er be breathed to me
Now. . . It is strange ; the sound of those dear words
So long unwonted, thrills my very soul.
And yet, alas ! I looked for no more love—
Enough : I have had enough !—all over, now. . . . . .
But I have been in a delicious trance
Where thou, unheeding little babbler ! thou,
Incarnate sinless beauty wonderful,
Hast clambered o'er me, gleeful prattling ; played
With my loose hair, and peeped inquisitive
Into my unclenched hands, to count their rings.
Thou didst "make friends with me"—yes, at first
       sight !
What was it drew thee to me in my smile ?
It was a sad smile, and not meant for thee—
They were not pleasant thoughts that called it forth ;
My spirit's dream was far from scenes like this—
But thou didst, uninvited, rash break in,
Running up to me, as by accident,
And then, half shy as at a stranger, half
Rejoicing to have found a playmate here
Instead of solitude—didst hide thy face
Upon my shoulder.—And I cannot tell
How long thou hast shared the mossy couch with me,

Beneath the shade of these retiring trees
Where I, reclining wearily, alone,
Had sought an hour of respite, unobserved,
To give myself up to my desolate grief.
But thou incessantly, with charming wiles
Hast won my meditation back to earth
(It was not straying heavenward, before !)
In spite of me, thou hast forced me to take heed
Of thy gay interruptions.   Yet, withal,
Thou canst not cheat me wholly of myself—
The very contrast of the light and dark
Which thou unwittingly intrudest on me
Must be by me the more acutely felt
That it is inconceivable by thee !
Ah ! child !   Thou hast not tasted of that tree
Whose fruit is knowledge of the evil.   Thou
Beholding me in moments whose distress
May have no witness (for whoever knows
The meaning of such anguish, knows too well
The cause of its keen sting)—wert thou with me
When I am free to shed remorseful tears
Whose bitterness I hide not from myself,
Yet to myself may not acknowledge oft,
But only when alone—thou, couldst thou look
Upon those tears—wouldst never understand ;
Wouldst see the suffering, but not the sin :—
Unto the pure all things, indeed, are pure !
It seems as they had power—would that might be
As true as beautiful—it *is* almost so—
To purify all human things, with stain
However vile, which innocently they
Received into their blessed confidence.

I, in full knowledge of the barrier drawn
Between me and the virtuous human kind,
I, without plaint, the edict recognise
Of my rejection from society ;
I without protest do accept its ban—
Yet feel as though some secret, higher law
Unrecognised, to thy pure spirit were known,
Unto whose sanctity I might appeal
For its protection.   Yea, thy innocence,
Reversing by its privilege divine
The sentence on my head,—doth plead my cause
And yet itself give judgment ;—I, bent down
In my humility, do hear it pronounce
Acquittal.   Ah, its voice is very low ;
Only to ears whose hearing by sharp pangs
Of sorrow has been made quick, perceptible.
The world is utter deaf to that sweet voice ;
There is enough of music, and of stir
From the war-marches and triumphal songs,
To deaden it.   Only to those like me,
The captives, bruised, and mourners, trodden down—
To us it penetrates : and oh ! to us
What sweetness in its compensation dwells !
We have our consolations, dreamed not of
By those who need them not.—How oft I feel
The dumb compassion of inanimate things.—
The beauties of free Nature :—unto me
Their inarticulate converse renders more
Than to her stainless, glad communicants.
A subtle fellow-feeling, part expressed,
But more withheld, and dim conjecturable,
Is by my lonely spirit, in its moods

Of deep dejection, secretly perceived
In the mysterious stillness of the boughs,
In the crimson-steeped radiance through the veil
Transfused of far-off, sunset filtering clouds ;—
It tells me, that at least there is *one* fane
So sacred, that all worshippers' who draw
Together, to partake its holy rites,
Must in their common reverence be merged
In one abasement.   All ; the righteous proud,
The highest in earth's moral-order grade,
Must bow before this holiness from far,
With the despised and reprobate ; yes, all
Unto the spirit of this purity,
This mystery of Nature, be profane.
Yet unto all, the sacred precincts wide
Are open—condescension infinite
Receiving all the human erring race
Into blest commune with its sanctity ;
Inspiring all with the same pious awe,
Breathing one absolution over all ! . . .
Such is the solace that my spirit draws
When, in deep-wooded groves, or on the hills
Where the fresh breeze is sickened by no scorn
Of city's breath ; or, in blest intervals
Between the summer and winter of toilful years.
Beside the eternal sea, the symbol grand
Of sorrow conquering and absorbing joy,
I steal away, and hide me from the crowd,
The mingling of my foes and crueller
False friends—then do I triumph over them,
Over myself—my past, my sins, my woes,
My wrongs, in one proud pæan of contempt !

. . . Another solace oft I love to seek ;
Unfailing is it, though too soon it grows
Wearisome ;—'tis the comfort that I find
When on my breast I yearningly caress
A little playful kitten ; with soft paws
That pat my cheek confidingly, with eyes
Large, yellow, innocent, that gaze at me
With a quaint, wondering look sometimes ;—or yet
I fancy it—with pitying tenderness ;
The little sportive creature never tires
Of gambol at my feet, or on my knee ;
And, as I stroke the round and silky head,
Or smoothly lay back the small upstart ears,
The thought comes to me almost peacefully—
How to this little kitten I am all
That the most stately lady, the most fair
And prudent matron, could be ; how none else
Could take my place, perhaps, to this one small
And inconsiderable creature.—No,
The faithful, loving, gentle little friend
Stops not to make inquiries, to review
My antecedents ; danger is there none
That this true friend, this undiscerning friend
May ever slight me, at the whispered word
Of scandal—or forsake me, or look cold
With haughty censure.—Such is my soul-aid
Derivable from soulless animals.—
And just at first, O beauteous little child !
Such seemed the meaning of the transient calm
Which thy consoling prettiness, on me
So artlessly displayed, threw o'er my soul.
For thou art all as trusting ignorant,

As guileless.—Yet the human soul in thee
Shall, with the labouring years, expand into
The consciousness, the knowledge, and the dread
Which are the shadow cast by hateful guilt
On fearful innocence.—To look on thee,
And feel how thou wouldst loath me, hadst thou but
Attained to thy full heritage !—the world
Shall put thee in possession of it, soon—
Too soon ; and then thou shalt discriminate,
Even as those around thee, who would point
At me with horror—and then drop their voice
In speaking of me, if they knew *thee* near ;
And to thy curious questions, or the prayer
Earnest imploring, whereby thou mightst seek
To deprecate their anger, when they found
Thou hadst been with me—they would shake the head,
Sigh, and perhaps in silence pray for thee ;
But never would they let thee hear my name,
Or touch upon this little episode,
This hour we spend together ; they would watch
Anxiously, day by day, waiting to see
If any faint remembrance followed thee
Of our chance meeting. . . . . O ! they need not thus
Distract themselves with paltry, vain alarms !
I know, this little stolen happiness,
This little joy which thou hast found with me,
Is harmless to thy soul : I would forego
For thy sake, love, this blessed, soothing dream :—
I would relinquish this illicit joy,
Did I not feel that even in my arms
There could not be contamination, yet,
For thee,—for such as thee.   Ah no, not yet.

In a few years—few years to me! God grant
It may be many years!—thou, too, shalt be
Woman; and then, thy hand in touching mine
Were sullied—thou at least wouldst deem it so;
I know not if it would be so indeed;
If the mature soul, keeping its first truth
And unsuspicious guilelessness—might not
Be mercifully to itself exempt
From the mysterious law of moral taint
Whereto association with the accursed
Condemns the baser, more degraded soul.—
I know not; it is not for me to judge;
The culprit may not be interpreter
Of that law's stringency, by which is made
The award of his perpetual banishment:
I bear my exile, and I murmur not.—
But *thou* art not yet subject to the code
Which regulates world-virtue's intercourse;
Thou art beyond its pale as much as I:
But thy exception is not mine—alas!
Fatal distinction! Thou art on *this* side;
Not yet admitted into citizenship
Of the august republic.—I—beyond—
Cast forth—deprived for ever of my claim
To its fraternity. Ah! well for thee
Could'st thou protract thy lingering without:
But, once the bounds are open unto thee—
God help thee evermore to keep within.
May'st thou be never tempted by the fiends
That lured me, fool, to clear the definite line
Of that reserved enclosure. *Once without,*
That line is ne'er repassed; no entrance more

Shall ever to entreaties of despair
Be granted ; penitence, of no avail,
Soon learns to dash away its piteous tears.
We outcasts walk, at last, with firmer tread
Upon the precipices, that reveal
Sudden abysses 'neath our devious path,
Than those who dwell in safety—as they call
Their temporary guaranty :—who knows
How soon its talisman shall prove to them
As useless as to us ?   At sorest need
Their vain security may fail them ; so,
In constant trembling of uncertainty,
And sense of danger dimly understood,
They walk with painful steps, 'midst their restraints
Guarded imperfectly,—not guided :—*We,*
After the first, irrevocable slip,
We grow sure-footed.—O, these awful thoughts
That never cease to haunt me, *will* recur.
Is even thy pure presence impotent
To exorcise their magic ?   Hast thou then
No counter-charm to my own spirit's ban ?
Must I be still reminded what I am,
When I had feigned by thy enchanting aid
Illusion so delightful ?   Must these taunts
Of my tormenting demons even encroach
On the dear hour that would once more of peace
Make restoration to my memory ? . . . .
And thou dost lay thy innocent sweet lips,
Thy rosy, warm, soft lips, unto my cheek. . . . . .
How long, how long it is since human touch
I have borne without a shudder. . . . Yet thine eyes
Look up to mine with full, frank, asking gaze :

It seems that they must read mine through, as clear
As angel glances, or the sight of God.—
Long have I steeled myself, to look with stare
Of bold defiance into all the eyes
The mocking, cold eyes of the cruel world,
That turn their questioning insolence on mine
And seek from my impassive face to read
My heart's most deadly secret : such demands
I can meet daring—parry shame by scorn.
But thine appealing look ! O, shouldst thou give
Expression to the tender, wondering dread
That all but speaks from those sweet wistful eyes
(Some intuition, wiser than the guess
Of pitiful suspicion, and more true
Than sneers of slander, must be hidden there),
If thou shouldst ask some question, ask it out
With mild simplicity, that straight should probe
My guilty consciousness.—What could I say ?
My eyes must droop from thine ; and from the clasp
Of thy small, clinging hands around my neck,
I shrink away—Ah ! had I paused, as now,
Once, at the gaze imperative of eyes
Less holy— hesitated, or opposed
Resistance less impulsive and more strong
To their fell fascination, which doth work
Even now—even now—as long as my spoilt life !
Had I but shrunk—*No :* back into these thoughts
I will not suffer me to wander now.
Let me forget, one moment ; let me feel
As but a moment since, when thy embrace
Startled me into the delusion sweet
That I might be even as a child, with thee !

Surely, my heart is dead now to all love
As well as to all hate ; I have achieved
That victory o'er my passion, in revenge
For its persistent injuries : I have learnt
With absolute indifference to regard
All men, requiring in return no less
From men to me.   But thou, bright little one,
Thou hast a spell from which I have no power
To fend myself ; it charms my heart once more,
And though I dare not open it to thee,
Though I must hold it closed to thy fair love,
Thou yet reveal'st to me the springs concealed
Whose pent-up waters have not lost their force ;
They might rush out once more, in surging flood
Of warm affection, overwhelming all
Their barriers, were they once unlocked . . . But thou
Who art the first to have that dangerous power
Since one who, ruinously, long ago
Wielded it o'er my will, to my own hurt —
Thou hast nor skill nor will to wield it so.
Thou teachest me to know my heart ; to find
A truth there that I blush not to confess
To my own soul ; though unto others, *now,*
I may not candidly this truth avow
More than I was permitted *then* to hide
That self-avowing truth, whose pitiless
Betrayal was my spirit's blight.   To thee
I will not breathe this truth, though thou dost seek
Its confirmation by thy prayerful look.
The love thou askest of me I may not give ;
And yet I cannot, though I would, withhold
Its fulness from thee ; though thou shouldst not seek,

It were compelled. *I love thee :* I, whose love
Must ever be a demon, to all those
Who cope with it ; because it once hath been
Endued with its own curse, which clings to it
As did the leprosy to him who dared
Unhallowed contact with the infected lure
Which harmlessly passed by the holy one
Who, resolute in godly strength, declined
Its proffered bribes.—Let not my leprosy
Cleave unto thee—Be spotless from my curse ! . . . .
. . . " Give thee a kiss ! "   Nay, child !—Upon my lips
Yet dwells that poison—God preserve thee from
All such contagion ! . . . . I must leave thee now. . . .
" Will I not come again ? "—What ! thou dost weep
Already !—Thinkest thou to have found so soon
A friend ?—Ah well !   In even so short a time
Hath many a soul found its immortal foe,
Being by attraction irresistible
Impelled to recognise the affinity
Which draws it on most surely to its doom !
In just as short a time, the fateful flash
Hath oft illumed the groping consciousness
To swift perception of the glittering thread
That long o'erhead had floated unsuspect ;—
Then, at one moment's impetus, the grasp
Is ventured.—And that thread becomes a clue
Leading inevitably evermore
The wanderer through the darkness unrelieved ;
It never can be shaken off ; it winds
About his feet, entangling them ; and so
By its deceptive guidance, henceforth on
Leads him—on—on—on—onwards to the cleft

Predestined for his fall . . . O ! blessed tears !
Sweet child tears, wherein can no omen dwell
Of evil. —Dost thou weep to let me go ?
Canst thou so quickly love me ?   Is the love
Of innocence so quick to be aroused,
That is not goaded by a wrathful Fate ?
Ay !—but it is as quick to be forgot !
It hath no link with consequences dire
Which, once the spring be touched, close fast upon
Their victim ;—it is not a lovely snare,
From which escape is hopeless.   O, thy love
To me, is not to fear ;—'tis not *black love.*—
That blackness which doth line the unfathomed gloom
Of God's black hate. . . . Yes, love me, if thou wilt,
Just for this little moment ; love me, weep !
The love that parting kills is of no worth
For weapon in the warfare devils wage.—
Thou wilt forget me, all as easily
As thou dost shed these tears ; as easily
As I, who weep not, smile : falsely I smile ;—
As thou dost truly weep ; and yet, thy tears
Are far more transitory than my smile ;
That passes with me where I may not weep !
. . . . My darling !—No, I must not come again. . . .
That I have had, for this once, access to thee
Is by some chance—some strange mistake.   Ah, no !
Thou hast a mother ; she will keep thee from
All danger of companionship like mine,
Trust me, *now*, while it cannot do thee ill.—
But there must come a day, when all the aid
Of watchful love—the tenderest support
Shall lose its safe-guard ; there shall be no shield

To ward from thee the fiery ordeal
Which thy soul's adversary, the malign
Devil—or God—may have ordained for thee :
Then, to the strength of thy own spirit's mail
Must thy salvation be entrusted ; then
With arms which none can wield for thee, must thou
Brave the encounter—pass through it alone,
And wear eternally upon thy head
The laurels snatched by thy own valour—else
The brand of irretrievable defeat !—
Ah ! shouldst thou in that conflict ever stake
Thy happiness, thy honour—if it be
That in its issue thou must lose thy all—
God hear my solemn adjuration ! grant
That thou and I may meet again ! O, then
Will I remember, for *thy* sake, this hour
Whose blessedness, to thee lost as to me,
Shall then from thy remembrance faded be.
What thou hast been to me—refreshment blest
Restoring to my languid soul the draught
Of my lost youth, of heavenly purity,—
That cannot I, for all my grateful love,
My tender yearning for thy weal, to thee
Render :—But there may be some service sweet
Of recompense that I can do thee.—When
The world expels thee, and all sympathy
Turns from thee in thy desperate hour of need,
While yet thy heart is human sensitive,
Before it has grown hard, inured to guilt ;
When the first stroke of thy great punishment
Bewilders thee ; when thou art stunned, confused,
Scarce comprehending all the agony

Of thy life's broken future.—Come to me !
Lean thou thy head upon me, trustingly,
As now thou dost ; and look me in the eyes
With the same confidence :   I will repay
Then, if I may, this moment.   I, grown old
In the sad wisdom that experience brings
(The saints say that experience is but wrought
By tribulation.—So is it with me !)
Will give thee all of comfort that I can ;
Will lavish on thy bowed head such caress
As thy own mother, if she could forgive,
Might not unshrinkingly accord ; will hear
The story of thy wretched wrong and woe
Without a look, a gesture of reproach :—
Or, what thou wouldst not tell, will patient spare
To thy abashed and faltering speech ; will take
Thy weary form into my arms, that then
Shall seem a haven from the evil world,
A welcome rest, care-burdened one !—My heart
Shall open then its record, so fast sealed
That only unto grief like mine its bonds
E'er shall give way—but I will tell *thee* all
—All that has made me what I long have been,
And yet now I have lived through all ! . . . I will—
. . . . O God ! forgive me this wild vow ! Sweet child,
I have been near—so near, I tremble now
To think it—near to wishing *that might be*,
In my rash craving for the possible boon
That thus were mine to render thee. . . Oh, no !—
Rather than contemplate the fearful thought
An instant, that thou mayst be yet like me,
Down even to level with my sympathy,

Instead of far up on the heights, wherefrom
Thou shouldst look and spurn me in my grief,—
Rather than that, God take thy pure young life
And rescue it from a mere possible breath
Of ignominy.—Ah! but thou must toil
To struggle free from the assailing mire
Through whose defilement must all life drag on;
And though thou be of might to assert thy will,
And foil the demons laying wait for thee—
Yet, with what frightful wounds thou mayst come
    through
Thy battle; with spent strength, and deathly pain,
And awful weariness. Thou mayst break thy heart
In keeping pure thy hands. O heaven! the lot
Of those that love and live is terrible!
I would that thou wert saved from it; I would
That thou shouldst die!—O darling!—that were best;
I pray God for thee, that thou soon mayst die!
Why did not holy lips breathe o'er my head,
When I was pure as thou, the prayer which I,
With lips polluted, now breathe over thine?
Might I have passed away from life, with smile
Of parting-greeting to the gentle face
Of that dear mother, who did fondly stoop
To look upon the child who lay so still
Upon her breast—while she strange guesses made
Of the angel-dreams that kept my eyelids closed—
O had my life so ended!—Now I had been
An innocent dead child;—not yet perhaps
Wholly forgotten, but in loving hearts
Leaving a dim, dead, fragrant memory.—
Now, when I die, I shall be soon enough

Forgotten ; but my fame lives with my life,
And will not leave me to oblivion. . . . .
. . . . That laugh! that little gurgling laugh!—it seems
To give the lie to my dread earnestness ;
The sparkles in thy merry eyes, that shine
Through the tear-clouds, that have not vanished
    quite. . . .
O little one ! I will not look on thee
Longer—I cannot. Dearest, say goodbye ;
Now I must go. . . Yes, yes, my hand is cold. . . .
Thy nestling fingers round it close again
After the first start. . . . Now again, that burst
Of uncontrollable, exuberant mirth ! . . .
How little canst thou read my answering laugh !
Thou deem'st it flows from like light-heartedness.
Even to my ears its sound falls musical—·
Although I know the note whereon 'tis struck.
Yes—I have taught myself the graceful art
Of laughter—practised spontaneity !
My merriment is always at command.
They speak, astonished, of my levity—
They say, I have become so frivolous—
Wonderful, in regard unto the weight
With which my life is laden : it should be *crushed.*
No ! it is gifted with a self-recoil
Whose power protects it 'gainst the rudest shock.
My bearing shall not wantonly betray
The lasting sorrow preying on my heart.—
And yet—thou showest me that my boast is vain ;
With thee, I lose my cunning ; my gay tones,
My chosen modulations, faintly break :
It will not ring, my voice ; thou art too quick,

keep time together. . . . Dearest little pet
Let me go.—I *must* leave thee. . . . O ! farewell !

KNIGHT ERRANTRY.

"WHO art thou, O warrior staunch and bold,
In arms and in mien like the knights of old?
. . . O errant knight ! Hear this warning told—
    Those who would *dare* must *bear*."

"O vainly thy boding words are said !
I have challenged Life : on my fearless head
Have fallen the bolts of her fury dread—
    Let me dare, who so well can bear !

"I have chosen for watchword—it glitters here
On the pennon that waves from my champion spear,
That beckons onward my bold career— : —
    They who *will bear* may *dare*.

"This is the warfare I choose for me :—
To wrest the great secret from destiny !
. . . I have proved my weapons in agony—
    I *dare*—I *can bear!* . . . I dare !"

EWIGES SEHNEN.

Alas! May nought than immortal be?
Not even the anguish of memory? . .
'Tis strange, when so long all my joys are fled,
That I weep, at last, for a sorrow dead!
O! the very *pain* that so much has cost
Is too precious to be unmourned lost;
'Tis the dearest sadness, to be bereft
Of the only relic my bliss had left—
The bliss that so long since went from me;
But I vowed that its fondness should deathless be;
No other gladness should ever take
The vacant place, for my lost love's sake;
There was nought that again could bid me care. . .
But the *Past*—all my hopes were buried there,
And my eager joys; so, resignédly
I turned me unto their memory—
For that could not die; its low voice cried
With a constant wail; through my life did glide
Like a ghost, the one thought that hence must be
My haunting spirit eternally.

O! the world's current hath not ceased to flow;
It holds no pause, for my stagnant woe;
And I have drifted on with the stream
Moving unconscious, as in a dream—

No interests new, no joys, no cares
Have drawn my sympathies unto theirs—
The terrible loneliness hath still
Clung unto me, as it ever will ;—
But the wild regret, that absórbéd me
With passion of long intensity,
Has slow relaxed ; and my life drifts on
Away—away—from that bliss far gone—
And the haunting thoughts, in the din and the strife,
Are silenced ; the life of my seeming life,
The inner, the only real to me,
Is merged in the outer reality.—
And I cannot, except by respites brief
Luxuriate in my cherished grief ;
No longer, familiar as of old
Doth my soul with the Past secret converse hold. . .
And I miss the spectre, in the end,
That filled the place of my dearest friend ;
When that place is void, I would call back there
Even pain, that kept it from being bare,—
That held it from all intrusion free,
Sacred, though desolate, unto me :—
Now, that the sanctified ground once more
Be common, and open as before—
Free for all trifles to enter there
And efface the dark traces—I cannot bear !
O ! when every holy sign is gone
From memory—leave it alone, alone !
It cannot, it must not be cast away—
For the faded joy's sake let it stay ;
Though the hope that died, should it once more wake
Could not stir the heart that it failed to break—

Could not cause one pulsing to flutter higher,
Nor call back one moment of fond desire—
Though all that so passionate real did seem
Have sunk lifeless cold, as a vague, past dream. . .
O ! let it be kept *as a dream*, apart—
Hallowed in thought to the musing heart,
Like the dreams of blest childhood so far away,
That pale from the mocking glare of the day. . .
O ! worship it unto Eternity ! . . . . .
Nay !—the mortal doom ! . . . O, that may not be ! . . . . .

Alas ! My sweet grief I in vain recall :
Well may I weep ; for it was my all.
No joy, no sorrow, can move me now—
My listless soul at no shock doth bow :
I may not hope, and I cannot care. . . .
All, all is past ! . . . O, is this—despair ?

LIFE.

We could not, if we would, say what is *Life*:
Strange, fearful essence of a thing divine.
We could not say whence comes each gentle breath
Which, as a soft wind from another laud,
Rises, and falls, and passes fleet away. . . .
Yet, life is not a vapour, to be dispelled
By a chance moment in impalpable space.
'Tis something, holy in its mystery,
Unconquerable in its inherent power,
Mighty and deep, with an instinctive force
Self-moving—self-existent—self-enduring—
Perpetuating itself through all the strife
Of the opposing forces ; undismayed
By all its contradictions—evil, and death,
Fear, weakness, ignorance ; unsubdued by Fate,
Undaunted by negation ; and over doubt
Despair and error ever triumphing. . . .

Time cannot cincture Life.   A record brief
Of transientest appearances is all
Within his limits comprehended :—Sudden,
Scornfully flinging from her his frail fetters,
The exhaustless soul-life sweeps beyond his bounds,
Leaving within his tremulous grasp no clue
To guide his gropings after her trackless flight.

O Life ! sublime and awful !—What art thou ? . . .
Stretching forth grandly o'er all time and space,
From ages remotest past to vistas dim
Of possible shadowed-forth futurity ;
Thou endless universal ! whose elements
Compared with that vast whole which they compose
—The individual to the infinite—
Seem so poor, little, imperceptible,
Dying away as swift as they arose,
Each vanishing from the arena wide
A brief, a stifled breathing—fading away
One into another, as the years roll on
And generations pass and are forgotten. . . .
Yet is the life-flood ever proudly pouring
Itself impetuous forth ; unchecked, still moving—
The one, eternal force—to which all others
Yield—all contained in, all resolved to—thee !

O Life ! thou light of Time's dark chaos ! How
Dost thou awaken in the mortal breast ?
Whence dost thou kindle that ecstatic flame
Which burns, more brightly ever, to no end ?
How dost thou enter this material world
And animate it by thy impulses ?
Where springs thy motive-power, which ruleth all
The universe—owning *thee* master, thee
Glorious, triumphant, blesséd, godlike Life !

We know not, yet :—we do not know thee, Life ;
We wait to know thee, yon the realms of Time,
In thy blest native sphere—on those pure shores
Where mists of Death ne'er baffle the supreme sight.

The earth-bound spirit, imperfect and warped as yet,
Must shrink to contemplate with giddy gaze
The mystery of that life beyond itself
Wherein all spirits have being ; origin
Of all existence, into which back flow
Its never-ending streams ; the life which never
Changes, nor pauses—strives, nor is assailed ;
Subject to no conditions—omnipotent.
We know not of the life the soul can bear
In the completeness that she shall attain
When her high destination is revealed.
We know not of the life *that is to come,*
Receiving our rapt spirits (after the pause
In which their bondage ceases) into itself,
Bliss of existence inconceivable !
Glorious development of the infinite force
Lying latent, and but partially concealed,
In the frail germ entrusted to the charge
Of struggling, unassured *Humanity.*
Who, from this faint and doubtful first assay
Of her immortal powers—anew endowed
With strength unfailing—riseth invincible
Above all limitations—beyond the sense
Of her own insufficience—perfected
Into the fulness of—*Eternal Life !*

FIRST LOVE.

(*Entered Apprenticeship.*)

I HAD just left school ; so I was not a school-boy ;
    Was ready to go into life ; and the way
I was taught to know the world—my first lesson,
So eagerly rushed at, was this—a love lesson :—
    Given to me in a " motherly way. "

She was a maiden ; fair, slim, stately—
    A year or two out of her teens, they say ;
I did not think, was she younger or older ;
I did not see that a boy might not love her,
    Or dream *she* could love in a motherly way.

I did not mean to fall in love with her ;
    But I was pleased that she deigned to play
With a cavalier so young and so simple,
When she accepted my acts of homage :
    (She took them, it seems, in a motherly way !)

Boys are vain : I was not quite so presuming
    As to fancy I could be helper or stay,
Or give to her all she would want from a lover ;
Yet it seemed that she liked to have me follow her,
    My patroness sweet, with her motherly way !

She treated me as no child : I was flattered
　　—Spite of misgivings from day to day—
At finding her put on the same little coquetries
That she assumed with her whiskered admirers,
　　For me :—to call *that* a motherly way !

Once I fixed my eyes long upon her—
　　Too long for such warm glances to stay ;
I was down at her feet, looking up at her ;
She turned her face from me, would not look down to me
　　—Truly, a very motherly way !

She laid her soft little hands on my shoulder—
　　Tenderly, gently their light touch lay ;
I never stopped, to think did she know it ?
To wonder, whether she thought *I* knew it ?—
　　I did not feel it a motherly way.

I dared to ask, would she let me kiss her ?
　　She moved not from me, nor pushed me away ;
Only she blushed, and her eyes drooped a little ;
And she let a half-smile on her lip-curves linger—
　　. . All, of course, in most motherly way ! . .

Every charm, every grace that she had, all her prettiness
　　Would she show off, merely on me ; display
The wonderful power her eyes had of changing,
In sudden brightenings, in wistful effusions—
　　Indescribably :—O ! in a "motherly way ! "

Her woman's wit dazzling she laid out before me ;
　　Brought her force of mind to bear on me ; nay,

Did not grudge from the stores of her deep soul-treasure
To murmur bewilderings cf mysteries, of secrets
    Too dangerous to touch on, in motherly way.

Why would she drift into subjects so earnest
        With me, if she looked on me fit but for play ?
Like the boys she teased, and the girls she petted ?
O ! her voice in speaking to me, rang—faltered—
        Sank low and faint ; *not* in motherly way.

She feared not to seize my impulses ; mould them,
        Youth's strong-springing thoughts, as they rose ;
            to her sway
She fashioned the tendencies, principles, feelings
Whose influence must bend my whole life-course ;—
            took on her
        Such onus, for sake of her motherly way.

        .   .   .   .   .   .

I heard her answer her brothers, laughing,
        (" You will flirt with even a boy ! " said they)
—" Flirt ? not a bit of it !—He is good fun for me ;
Really, I take quite an interest in him—
        Just, you know, in a motherly way ! "

. . . I was a boy, after all ; she a woman
        I ought to have known it ; she knew it ;—yea
She did not forget herself.—I, for my folly
Had my hard stroke ; learnt its moral, unplaining—
        That was what came of the motherly way !

LAST LOVE.

(Sequel to "Entered Apprenticeship.")

———

GOOD-BYE, dearest !   My heart calls after,
And follows you far.   You think it is done,
Your love-dream ; you know not my heart is won,
You cannot listen into its laughter.
Short shall this parting be—soon past ;
And then—I come back. . . . and own to you all: I am
    yours, at last.

I need to be wooed : it is women's doing ;
Their own the blame, if my faith is gone
In reflections of my own love-gazes on
Their pretty stare.—Of that kind of wooing
I have had enough.   Such meaningless eyes
Have looked me through to brief fascination, with
    simpers and sighs.

I have been a gone coon so often : the breaking
Of hearts I have learnt and unlearnt in a day ;
Have trifled two or three hours away
In one evening, with two or three styles of love-making:
Have practised on different subjects :—the same
I have found with them all : at next meeting, they
    quite have forgotten my name !

Without a thrill, in seizing or dropping,
Many a careless hand have I kissed ;
Praiséd the brightness of many eyes ; but no mist
Has risen into them, shyly stopping
The compliment—coolly asked by a look—
I can read, unembarassed, the face of a bold
coquette, as a book.

But you !—I can even detect the throbbing
Of the fingers you lay on my arm so soft ;
You lean on me always so lightly ; and oft
In the quick caught breath I fancy a sobbing,
As you half retract the low words you say—
I have to bend down so close, to be sure ;—that
frights them away !

I am sick—yes, downright sick, of love-making ;
Heartily tired, at last, of play :
I cannot play at it with you ; your way
Is so strange—your innocent earnest-taking.
There is more to you in love than " high art."
A *conquest* is not, to you, good payment as price of
a heart.

It spoils all fun ; for you have no notion
Of fighting me with my own weapons ; the rest
Of women are all fair game ; nay, the best
They have had of it yet with me. My devotion
Is spent in this warfare of gallantry ;
I have met my equal before ;—but you are too
much for me.

You call up all the old chivalrous feeling,
You grave little darling! that many a day
In the long years past I have mocked away.
How much there was left for your revealing
In the depths of my unstirred, stagnant heart
I could not have deemed.—Emotion made me
 tremble to part!

You believe yet in the object of living;
The dream of existence is real to you.
Pity to wake—as you soon must do
If I leave you alone to your fate; all giving—
And nought in exchange to be taken! So
Goes the lot of the trusting and simple—to teach
 them wisdom, I trow.

I have learnt it; the women have taught me.
Once, an ideal of womanhood
I had: I have lost it;—if ought as good
As your sweet perfection my triumphs had bought me,
I had not found so bitter to drink
The cup of revenge: betraying is sad as betrayal, I
 think.

I cannot be cynic with you. For passion
Capacity all is worn away;
But I feel my heart opening day by day,
In a tender, fatherly-brotherly fashion :—-
To love and protect you, your guide to be,
And have you cling to the rest of my life, is future
 to me.

—It can be.   A quiet home—affection
  Easing my calmed life of all its care—
  My little one nestling beside me there,
Her young life growing to my direction—
  Her thoughts, her hopes, and her will all mine—
  For that let the memory vanish of flirtations toasted
    in wine.

Let me drink to the joys of love at its truest,
  In the wine I drink at my own fireside,
  Where soon I shall lead you, a happy bride.
We will live retired, with friends of the fewest ;
  No *show* to disturb us ; no gaiety
  To break our peace ;—I have done with all dash, all
    mad levity.

I shall settle down.   We will live together
  Models of virtue, tasting home-bliss
  To the full. . . .   O, have you a guess of this ?
Does your fluttering heart muse this moment, whether
  I think of you after last night's good-bye ?—
  Send your thoughts in search of me !—trust them to
    reach me safe, by and bye.

Absence will test us.   I do not fear you ;
  Others may come with their vows : you will be
  Your own heart's keeper.   Keep true to me—
Guard your best love still for me ; . . . and near you
  Soon you will find me again,—to claim
  The beautiful gift you have taught me to prize.
    You will be just the same.

At my first step you will start ; our meeting
  Will scare away from your eyes the sad smile ;
  The rustle of my first kiss for a while
Will charm back the blush that rose for my greet-
    ing. . . .
  And what shall I say after that ? . . . After all
  I do not know ! . . . Ah, bewitcher ! *I love you—*
    You have me in thrall !

GLORIOUSLY FELL.

AGAINST the arched wall of the transept white
Rises a marble sculptured monument,
Commemorative of the fame of one
Who died in battle.   Flung beside his steed,.
In whom the throes of life's last agony
Are quivering, leans the warrior, sunk to earth,
His limbs relax ; scarce can the nerveless form
Support the head thrown back with straining gaze
To look where, closely nearing him, there speeds
The figure, strong and beautiful, of one
Superb and fleet—angel of Victory.
The solemn messenger, with hovering wings,
Droops toward the flaccid hand which stretches forth
Unto the wreath of bays suspended held
In the fair angel-hand, above the form
Of the dying hero.   On the extended hand
Death falls, prohibiting its mortal touch.
And the wreath floats for ever, in that pause,
Above the brow in death immortalised. . . . . .
Thus speaks the marble eloquence ;—below
Is graven in the stone " Fell gloriously."

And in the spirit awful sanctified
Of the solitary gazer, who stands long

In contemplation of the mystery
Presented in such symbolism divine,
Heroic aspirations rise in flood,
Transforming, with their suddenness, the soul
From its wonted state of slow conformity
To the requirements of the sordid world,
Its gentle acquiescence in the life
That with its dictum so hath worked upon
The imperiousness of its first native bent,
As to quite tone it down, and smoothly check
The enthusiasm that once was holy fire.—
The compromise with practicality
Its trammels loosens now, unwarily;
The youthful ardour, not all calmed away,
Upsurging sweeps before it in its rush
All prudence of the faculties matured,
And plays the master.   In the swift-freed thought
Ideal anticipations reawake
Of glory possible, of fame to seek,
Of a career elect, a future wooed,
Of a vocation claiming all the power,
The love, the passion, and the sacrifice,
The patience, and the energy of life.
No danger seems an obstacle ; no count
Of risk can make him pause : no boding dread
Of long renunciation, of regret,
Of disappointment, or of failing end,
Can hold back his quick daring.   Only there
Where peril challenges, and scorn to be
Confronted, and suspense to be endured—
There seems the path worthy of his proud choice :
And if prophetic in his spirit looms

A warning of the terror imminent,
That cannot be escaped at last, he feels
In that high moment equal to the fate
Of meeting it—not quailing at its blight.
If after his struggle, when the end has come,
Breaking his chosen pathway—in the speech
Of men must live the record that he fell—
Let them, then say ". He fell," but stop not there:
His record be—" He fell—but gloriously." . . . .

Magic impulsion, strange constraining power
Of those inspiring words !—Strange meaning, words
Unblending.   Was it glorious, then, to fall ?
Was not the glory for the rest reserved,
Those who returned victorious, and who wore
Their laurel on the living brows ? . . Ah no !
Better to die : better to have the life
Finished to perfectness, triumphant end.
It is at death alone that angels come,
And hold out those celestial crowns of bays
Which never mortal-opening eyes may see.
The dying glance can see them, with its power,
Its clearness of far reaching vision brief.
Such vision renders all unfit for life
The sated eyes—as much as holy awe
Forbids renewal of life's scenes profane,
After the holy unction at the last
Hath been administered to him who waits
For rending of the screen before heaven's light.—
Best and most satisfying fate is his
Whose hand falls stiff in death ere he can grasp
The withering bays which earthly honour life.

For him the immortal bays are flourishing
That twine their wreaths unto his memory.

How many a glorious life is left uncrowned
Until the crowning moment comes with death !
Such of the noblest lives is epitaph,
" Gloriously fell." . . . .
　　　　　　　　　　How often is the fall
But measure of the height of the ascent—
How many a mountain summit, nearly scaled,
Glooms back stern satire on the aspirants
Who with the infatuate gaze of late despair
Behold it, lone and inaccessible
Towering in its cold grandeur, as they reel
From the unyielding precipice ; while far
Below, the myriads journeying through the plain,
Pursue their even round, saunter or crawl,
Rest when they will, and come unto the end
Of their appointed circle, having made
The passage round the threatening mountain's foot
Safely and peacefully—to find the end
Merely as the beginning.—O ! to fall
Means often but to have too short attained :
To aspire, stupendous, to the infinite,
And be by shackles of the finite tripped—
That is to fall.—Glorious it is to fall !
Most true, most holy end for yearning aims,
Fulfilment all-sufficient of the hopes
And sacred pledges of the most intense
And earnest manhood, in those thrilling words
" Fell gloriously." . . .
　　　　　　　　　　And here, in this most blest

Most solemnising presence of our fane,
This hero-temple ; here, the hallowing pledge
I take within my soul, and vow myself
To its observance with all loyalty,
All truth and deep attachment; changelessly
Constant to keep in view to my life's end
This martial-strong resolve that burns in me,
Whose utterance apotheosis finds
In the sublimely sculptured emblem there.
—For ever are we all at war with life ;
And, conquering or conquered, may not hope
To come back from the field, bearing our bays ;
So then, when soon or late disarmed I fall
Let it at least be gloriously. . . . O God !
—So rise the prayer I breathe in the pure name
Of the ultimate religion, that includes
The best, the dearest of all worships old,
The capability of all to come,
The whole of spiritual sympathies,
Whatever longings after Deity
Have purified men's thoughts, and raised their wills,
From time to endless ;—unreproved by doubt,
I, lifted now to rapturous reverence, pray
In that religion universal—God !
Be my pledge faithful kept, my service true,
Its end accomplished nobly, and my fight
Victoriously achieved by glorious fall !

KINDRED SPIRITS.

(Emilia Viviani to Shelley in absence.)

NEVER to meet again, we two have parted;
  Shall we to one another be no more?
It has been all then but a blissful dream; the brief
    illusion
  Faded, the *Real* is left—blank as before.—

No! not for that hath risen the glorious vision
  Flashing on my bewildered eyes the light
Which my despair, in aidless struggles with the
    dreadful darkness,
  Has passionately called—the blind for sight.

No more vouchsafed than a pure, transient gleaming
  O'er the gloom; but I will hold for ever dear
It has been :—yea: the concentration of the utter
    brightness
  Which comes, for once, to make all endless clear.

Can I forget? It hath no durance finite,
  That joy; not to be grasped, then let go by—
But, now *I know :* it was the Revelation, one-sufficient,
  At last, in response to my heart's wild cry.

Alone, so long, have I all vainly striven
  In grief, with questionings and perplexity,

Horribly—hopelessly—and yet not daunted : in one
    supreme moment
  The life-withheld transcendence is found—*in thee !*

Souls that have been so close, but once, are nearer
  —For all the distance that must come between—
Each to the other through Eternity, than those who linger
  In bonds where never parting may have been.

There is a wondrous sympathy inspireth
  Affinities in hearts which it doth move ;
Absence can loose not that strong charm that rules
    their separate throbbings,
  Nor null their union ;—it is *more* than love !

Love may be bann'd to us ; the blesséd solace
  Which others yearn for ;—to face together strife,
To lean upon each other, thus work out our unsolv'd
    destinies blended,
  Reading with mutual gaze the spell of life—

Deeming it were so, only ; and not knowing
  What sorrow, in compensation, teacheth me ;—
By reverent communing with sacred doom intimate,
    to interpret
  Aweless, her mystic and unscanned decree. . . .

The phantasms of our outward self,—at present
  Life keepeth them apart : as *Death* doth seem
To sever those Life's mockery held deluded yet :—
    known truly
  Life and Death are changes but of one fleet dream.

Both substitues of shifting shows unreal
  For the true substance that in soul doth dwell;
While *that*—enduring age through symbols inadequate
    —ne'er ceaseth
Resistless sole, all Being to compel.

Veiled by whatever form perceptible ; rendered
  In what entanglement of circumstance ;
The subtle power of the sweet influence, uncontrollable
  Moulds individual destiny—*not* chance.

Not chance !   Inevitably souls each other
  Sway and subdue, unchecked by space or time ;
Mingle, absorbing each other's essence ; inscrutably
    evolving
  Action, whose harmony is Fate sublime.

The guiding clues each of the other's being
  Coming in contact *once*—intricately
Are twinéd ; then, though courses devious draw them
    on to spheres far sundered,
  They evermore guard innate unity.

Too vast the scope of such wound fates for scanning
  Of mortal dazed conception ; mystery blest
Instinctive conscious but in the initiate ; cherished
    secret,
  By spirits whose force doth 'neath their semblance rest.

For them—the "might have beens" shall be translated
  Into the perfectness of one full speech ;
Lost glimpses of the unattainable—all comprehended
  In the wide sweep of one view of boundless reach.

Under all maze of thought, and deed, and passion,
  Souls yet keep true to their deep law divine ;
Through this life—incomplete phase of existence
    infinite—and beyond it—
  'Tis changeless—I *thine* only—and thou—*mine.*

FROM THE SECRET STUDIO.

Two Pictures.

NIOBE.

THERE stands she, stately cold, and queenly fair,
Encoroneted by her own dark hair ;
In the grey eyes, 'neath that cold brow divine,
Doth cold light ever without sparkling shine.
Man cannot guess from her cold smile unmoved
If ever she have hated, or have loved ;—
Nor from the cold, impassive hands, now pressed
Coldly upon the cold unheaving breast.
From those cold eyes long have the tears been gone ;
Those firm, cold lips no quiver lighteth on ;—
Yet on the erect, cold, marble-rigid head
Some awful weight of sorrow, heavy dread
Must once have fallen ;—and passed away again,
Having on memory an eternal pain
For burden left ; whence comes the stony stare
That from the Past looks ceaseless through the fair
Stone-cold and tearless eyes.   But what joys dead
Have stonily thus fixed the unbowed head—
May not be learnt ;—this only can be known,
By gazing on the face so fearful grown—
That there is loss whose weeping turns the heart to
    stone.

MEDUSA.

This is, indeed, the face that once hath been
So beautiful ; that now may not be seen

Without a blighting horror, that doth chill
The heart's warm life, and petrify the will.
But still, though no more lovely, all who dare
To gaze into it see that it is fair ;
Yea, that a terrible beauty therein lies—
In the unextinguished torment of the eyes ;
The anguish burning in the frenzied glare
Of those wide eyes, whose fury is despair,
Hath more of fascination than doth dwell
In tenderest love-glances ; yea, more fell
The look flashed from their deathless agony
Than the longing pain wherein sweet love doth die.
In the awed gazer's mind, wild doubts begin
Their haunting question—" Is it sorrow, or sin,
Whose fearful curse is on such beauty laid,
Whose evil breath hath good and gladness stayed ? " . .
The spirit that strives this mystery accursed
To interpret, answereth—alas ! . . . Sin *first*—
Then sorrow : as the one was, so must be
The other ; consequence eternally
Evolving retribution ; certain fate
From whose wound chains no struggle can extricate. . .
. . And ah ! be sure, those deadly eyes have not
Their cruel gleam without full payment got ;
The secret of their fatal power must be
In the incompensable cruelty
Dealt first to her :—So cruel are alone
Eyes whose own torture tortures into stone !
Some speechless wrong hath unto her been wrought
Wherein herself had part ; but shuddering thought
Can frame thereof no adequate conceit ;
The infinite pain no finite sense can meet.—

Light were it to divine, at least, her crime
Was love ; but of its forms, that through all time
Change, with new terrors—*which* it was that made
Her forfeit—ne'er to mortal soul afraid
Hath been revealed.   Such punishment as hers
Must cast its bane o'er the whole universe:
The measure of her suffering must be paid
By all who look on what she hath been made :—
Thus never shall on life the ancient curse be stayed.

IN PACE.

O ! RESTFUL sweetness that o'er me creeps—
   Till I fall back into the reverie
Where each regret, each reproach, charmed sleeps—
   O ! where, if not here, is peace for me ?
For me, for me, who have long forsworn
   The quiet and calm that in earth's joys seem ;—
Put them away, as at breath of morn
   We lay by the other self of dream.

There was a blessedness, long ago,
   That kept my heart so safe in its spell—
My very soul wonders now, to know
   How holy it was—yet I feel it well :
'Twas the innocence of my childhood's day ;—
   O, not its carelessness, not its mirth
Would I crave now—so long since passed away—
   But I dream here its truth come back to earth !

Once, all this calmness could weary me.—
   A restless longing, a deep desire
In the fling, in the changes of life to be,
   Stormed at my heart, till my blood was fire.
All woes, all wrongs on my soul to bear
   In the fight for pleasure, seemed me best ;—
Now the strife is o'er that I prayed to dare,
   How sweet it is to return to rest !

—To try every joy that life can give,
    And every sorrow, in losing more—
Until we deem that to cease to live
    Were acme of all that went before—
Then, when exhausted passion is low
    And languid, to be o'erwhelmed with bliss—
Passive to yield to its calm, strong flow—
Ah! what is happiness, if not this? . . . .

I may sink, in a trance that comes most nigh
    Unconsciousness of identity,
As I gaze on the lights that shift o'er the sky
    And glimmer opaline on the sea.
I cannot tire *now*—tire to gaze
    Through the fluttering tracery of my bower
On the lucent hues in their dim spray haze,
    And the clear green, flecked with the white foam
      shower.

My every thought with my eyes is led
    To the bright enchantment that keeps them bowed;
The flash of the silver sweeps that spread
    O'er the grey stretch under the morn-rent cloud.
While the measured monody faint doth greet
    My ear, from far, of the sighing waves
Plashing around the rocks at my feet
    Ere they leap high into the distant caves.

How blessèd, to let the sunlight stream
    O'er shade that the griefs of life have brought;
To lose the sense, in its glorying gleam
    Of the stain on feeling, and wish, and thought!

O, sorrow and joy alike may fade,
    Or mingle to tinge my soul's cloud-gloom ;
The shadows and lights whence its sky is made
    Are high yon the region of their doom !

THREE ASPECTS OF "THE LOVE OF WOMEN."

KATHLEEN'S INVOCATION.

(To St. Kevin, sleeping in his mountain cell).

. . . . AsLEEP! O, innocent, childlike, holy sleep!—
Dreamless: no haunting thoughts may dare disturb
The sweet serenity of thy tranquil brow.
'Tis I, methinks, who dream :—to stand so close,
Beside thee—look upon thy face again,—
And yet thou knowst it not.   I must not stir,
Else might my lightest sigh chance mar thy rest.
I would not have thee open thy calm eyes,
By penitential tears so purified
As only without shrinking to endure
The visions beatific which surround
With sacred spell thy blessed solitude,—
To encounter them with the detested sight
Of this face—this once loved, now hated face ;—
God knows how long its memory troubled thee,
And shut out from thy soul its peaceful thoughts,
Recalling to thee hours of sinful joy
With horrible temptation—till at last
Thou didst grow mighty, through thy fasts and prayers,
And fleshly torture, and the still more fierce
Conflicts with thy own human heart—with all
That once was as thyself, that now hath been
Cast from thee, leaving thee mere saint ;—and now,
As thy soul loathes the thronging fiends, who come

Around thee in thy hours of weakest strength
To assail thee with their impious mockery,
And peril thy salvation ;—as o'er them
Thou yet dost triumph ;—so thou loathest me ;
Dost triumph, so, o'er my forsaken love.
O ! never dost thou give one tender thought
To her, the lost through love of thee ; no more
Dost thou look back—for that were sacrilege,
I would not that thou wert so frail—upon
That expiate time when to each other we
Were all on earth—and that was more than Heaven !
No pity canst thou feel—(*that* were a sin,
Perhaps,—I must not wish it—) for my woes
That have outlived thine : thou hast Heaven on earth,
Now ; and between us there is fixed a gulf. . . .
O ! it is terrible !—I see thee still,
But with a cruel, ever maddening sense
Of separation, that of *death* beyond.
Thou art as far from me—as God ! And still
Like him, more fearful that thou art so near. . . .
Those hands, that lie so restful on thy breast
Folded, as in brief pause of wrestling prayer.—
Are they the very hands, warm flesh and blood
That once clasped mine ?—Seized them imperiously,
Compelling them to passionate caress ?—
That drew me fervently to thy embrace
Until our faces met ?—In that close kiss
How hot my lips felt thine . . . O Heaven ! those lips
On which there lingers now the softest smile,
Relic of thy unearthly musings. . . . . How
Couldst thou have deemed that there were danger yet
In my cursèd presence—all unfelt by thee,

The angel guarded ;—how should I have power
To break through that charmed atmosphere, that here
Shieldeth thee ?—if to fiends impenetrable
Much more to me, faint, trembling reprobate
Mortal, by mortals and immortals spurned,
Bearing my outward shame and inward grief
With an unbreaking heart ; yet from the spell
Of this thy holiness, shrinking in dread.
Thou needst not fear my desecrating hand
Touching thy own imploringly, to feel
The pulse responsive to its thrill once more.
Thy lips are cleansed : miue have once *tasted blood*—
And never ought can slake their thirst again.

. . . . Restlessly as I stray, roaming the haunts
Of that dear past, too falsely beautiful,
My feet are driven hither ; the steep path
To me in vain denies the access barred
To other wanderers ; lightly the ascent
I scale ; no terror holds me back :—and here
Beside thy desolate couch, by the lone crag,
Thy only shelter from the mountain blasts,
Thou silent watcher of the precipice
That lieth darkly down, far down below
The sullen guardianship of thy retreat—
Here do I crouch ; dizzy, and stunned, and faint ;
Stifling my frantic breathing, hushing down
The gasping throbs of my quick-leaping heart,
Lest they should to thy slumber chaste betray
Intrusion so unhallowed. . . . O ! it is
No cheat of hope that leads me thus to thee,
Luring me to renewal of the bliss

That but a little while ago—O long,
Long while !—My soul's life and its death between—
Was real :—for now, although its memory
Is all too vividly burned into me
To leave my heart erased of it an hour—
Now, it is more than past. . . If thou wert dead—
(Alas ! Alas ! Why couldst thou not have died ?
Then might my thoughts have followed thee to heaven,
And to find thee, my prayers had day aud night
Ascended tirelessly unto the saints—
And I had so been saved ! . . . .)—If thou wert dead,
And 'twere thy corpse thus coldly beautiful
Lying umoved before me—I were not
More still in my despair, more stricken mute
Before the solemn sight—than by the look
Of pure oblivion on thy sleeping face. . . .
If thou shouldst sudden wake, and see my eyes
Bent on thee—thou need'st start not from their gaze ;
There shines no more pleading reproach—no more
Importunate entreaty in these eyes
Forwept—which once were lighted by the glow
Kindled respondent in them by the flash
Of thy most ardent glauces.—Ah, fond light
Extinct for ever !—Dread no more its power
To dazzle thee—I feel, thou hast no part
In ought of earth,—white clothed in purity !

Thou unto holiness hast given up love :
And I for love have given up holiness.
Thou to thy soul's weal hast made sacrifice
Of me, and of thy love : . . . for thy soul's weal
Thee I resign—but ah ! not *love*—not love !

I have made sacrifice of my own soul,
And in return have but my guilty love.
And yet, that love, all bitter and accursed,
Without one sweet alleviation—reft
Of every solace, every soothing hope—
Is more to me than Heaven or holiness.
I would not part with one of its true pangs
For the eternal bliss of saintly souls ;
Nor render up my passionate memories
Of those few hours of sweet, sad heedless joy,
Though every one can count long, dragging *months*
Of torturing retribution.   All the pain
Of the eternity of suffering
Which must requite that bygone happiness
Is far outweighed by the surviving bliss
Of but one moment of enchanted love.—
One of those moments lived in thy embrace,
That cannot be recalled :—Not all thy vows
Of abnegation can undo its spell,
Nor from my heart efface its impress deep.
No penance, or of God or man devised
Can stamp it out.   No ! while my soul hath life
(Which, for its everlasting punishment,
Must be conceded,) nought shall wrest from me
The recognition in my spirit of thine,
The consciousness of what hath been.—Hath been ?
Nay *is* for ever.—Thou art mine no more,
And with the gladness which thou didst renounce
Is gone, perforce, my portion of delight—
But love, in sorrow immortalised for me
Hath now become my all in all.   And still
It must be so.   Through whate'er change henceforth

My demon-transformation draweth me—
This mighty, all-engrossing love must cling
Inseparable, to my identity. . . . .
I will teach devils what is human love
That cannot be extinguished by hell-fire ;
How, in the endless realm of sin and woe
Where penitence, they say, is even shut out,
And all the gentler feelings that still dwell
Here, in lost souls, are turned to passions fierce,
And horrible remorse alone may reign—
How even there Love can be conqueror,
Carrying his triumphs 'midst the loveless fiends.
My damnéd soul shall scornfully refuse
To bend beneath the rule of envious hate.
Through all the execrations blasphemous
Uttered against the blesséd—I alone,
Companionless in agony, will gaze
Up to the far Heaven from the infinite depths,
And see thee in thy rapture—unalloyed
By thought of my perdition—unperturbed
In the eternal ecstasy wherein
Thy heavenly adoration hath calm joy,
Enduring in a passionless repose
Of perfect satisfaction. . . . I will look,
Undazzled by the glories of the rays
Of the intense lustre—by the majesty
Of Godhead, awful frowning in its wrath
On the doomed sinner, all unterrified ;—
Look, through the ages, . . . only look on thee !
Enough for me, enough to bear me through
The unintermittent torture steadfastly,
Be knowledge of thy bliss celestial,

And contemplation of thy perfectness. . . .
After brief struggle, thou hast overcome ;
Wear ceaseless thou the crown of martyrdom,
So be it mine to bear its cross for thee
Now, and hereafter.   Thou art victor : I
Am vanquished ; and at my great victor's stroke
I bow submissive ; taking all the ills
He doth award to me, with worship meek ;
Kissing his feet, who has bound me as his slave
For all eternity—for it is He,
The mightiest, dearest master o'er the earth,
—Ay, and o'er Hell, whither I follow him :
'Tis love, the beauteous victor ; and since Heaven
Is banned unto his sway—I would not have
My portion there.   Rather weep out my life
Of vain regret—then, deathless, evermore
Consuming, not consumed, in flames of doom
Cherish my human love, my lovely sin—
Than share thy blessèd saintly state with thee ;
Dwell on for aye, like thee, in Paradise,
Absorbed in heavenly love, and God—not thee !
. . . Be thou, more glorious, victor over Love,
And as thy meed, take Heaven.—To me, leave Hell,
And quenchless love, and burning thoughts of thee. . . .

Ah ! but . . if it were thus : were we but so
Separate—thou in Heaven, and I in Hell—
There were not then this dull, this sickening pain
Longer for me ; which every dreary hour
Writhes round my heart, crushing it down even here.
O ! this is worse than parting !—thus to be
In the same life with thee, and know our souls

Severed irreparably.—Were my woe
Infinite, I could bear it ; as I will
With patience infinite, in the life to come.
But O ! to go back now into the world,
The laughing, joyous world, that once hath been
So beautiful for me ; and in the crowd
Of living, loving creatures, all alone
Struggle with my abiding curse of guilt—
Unworthy even to raise a thought to thee,
Yet with a restless yearning still impelled
To sink myself, with all my aching griefs,
In thy existence, which absorbeth mine
With placid, cruellest unconsciousness—
While thou, in thy proud sanctity, art held
So far aloof—unchanging, though so changed
To me, whom life nor death shall change for thee. . . .
Would *that* were at an end. . . . The end must be. . .
But in this waiting for it, surely, lies
The very essence of the bitterness
Of my atonement. . . . Ah ! methinks thy brow
Is troubled. . . . Is it but a passing shade ?
Is it, indeed, or does my frenzied brain
By its incessant, concentrated gaze
Feign the most faint reflection glimmering
O'er thy calm, sleeping face, of thy rapt soul ? . . . .
How often have I watched thy speaking looks,
Interpreting what words cannot declare
Of spirit-utterance, only love inspired . . .
Thou self once taughtest me the precious lore
—How strange, remembrance of it eagerly
Rushes back on me now—the secret truth
" That bodily contact of things animate

Set free in one another wondrously
Invisible—working forces ; which would then
With one another intermingle ; so
Upon the spirits in those bodies pent
Work mightily, with mutual influence." . . .*
What if it were, that yet some power might dwell
In that unseen current of sympathy
Opened mysterious once, between us both ?—
That merely through my nearness unto thee
That power might subtly manifest itself
And so, against my will, into thy soul
In its deep trance, some motion, drawn from mine
Might steal, and stir it ? . . . . Ah ! . . . What
  have I done
If that be so ? . . . What would I ?—Giddily
My reason pauses . . . Ah ! . . I shudder ! . . . . Now
I know not whether I shall make recoil
Or spring forth daringly :—to what ?—O ! now
Desperate resolve, like madness, seizeth me.
I am all overpowered by a strong might,
Rousing rhapsodic in me wild desire
That must, that will have vent. . . . O ! to bring back
By the illusion of one moment blest
The past ; O might it but restore to me,
This wretched me, the sense of thy embrace . . .
In the transition of that moment, I
Would meet with rapture my eternal doom ! . . .
Mightst thou but look once more into my eyes
—One last, long look—And take me in thy arms. . .
. . And fling me thence to death ! . . . .

* This idea taken from Scheffel's Ehehard.

Awake ! Awake !
My love ! My own !—I call upon thee ! Hear
For the last time my voice : no farther plaint
Shall startle thy lone stillness ; let it be
Henceforth profound, unbroken ; mortal voice
Disturb it nevermore.—But once, O hear !
Answer my solemn summons—Wake ! awake
Love calls to thee—O answer !—There is but
One answer—that is Death ! Wake ! Wake !—O wake!

———

NON TI SCORDAR DI ME.

(*The New Satanella.*)

" Do not forget me." . . . . But I did not speak. . . .
Ah me ! How often have I wondered, since,
Has *he* thought of that silence ? Called it back
To his remembrance half as tenderly
As I have murmured through those words of his,
Over and over, till they have become
A never silent echo, haunting still
The deepest hidden caverns of my heart ? . . . .
All my unspoken love was in my eyes ;
I know he read it there ; they grew so dim
With looking up in wild and fervent strain
Of passionate resistance—that no more
Could they behold him ;—Out to vacancy
Straight gazed they forward terribly, as if
The awful fascination of the ban
Which lay upon me, were compelling them
To look beyond the darkness of my soul,
Unconscious, and be blinded.   Nought I knew

Or felt, but fearful helplessness. . . . But he,
—Well I remember—looked into my face
With downward searching gaze, that seemed to take
Possession of it first—then pierce below
Into my inmost soul, and enter there. . . . . .
Will he remember, then, that look, as long
As I his voice?   The accents deep and low
Seem thrilling, even now, upon the air
Close to my ear ; their sound oppresses me
As doth the constant vision that some spell
Renders companion to the guilty one
To quicken his remorse ; seen but to him,
A secret burden weighing on his soul,
And well-nigh stifling it with crushing dread ;—
So does my spirit struggle with the charm
Which in its meshes yet entangles it ;
So does it seek in vain to free itself
From the perpetual haunting of that sense
Of the far, far gone past.   It *is* all gone—
It should be banished to forgetfulness.
By what right do our actions, rash and blind,
And in their *consequences* all too sure
Inflicting on us retribution full
For our ill-fated waywardness, live on
Even in their ghosts, with irrepressible power
To fetter and impede for e'er our wills?
Why can I live no more the present life,
Nor find the actual true again to me ?
Am I not all wildered, as in a dream,
Living an unreal life, beneath the curse
Of that e'er present past, that merges all
My faculties in its absorbing spell ?

That draws, mesmeric, my identity
Unto itself—dulling my energies,
Making one dread confusion in my soul ? . . .

That was our parting. Every lightest word
That passed our fated lips in such brief space
Is solemnised into a prophecy.
The thoughtless incidents—the sign scarce marked
At our strange meeting—the familiar thoughts
We interchanged—our converse, by dim sense
Of awe embarrassed—the omens vague that rose
In earnest speech—all were symbolical ;
All have been fearfully translated ; all
Have found fulfilment—ay ! the curse ! the curse,
Hath triumphed, and gained utterance over me.

Did I not recognise it in that hour
When Destiny came and looked me in the face
In answer to my challenge ?—I was proud,
Desperate, and defiant : I had looked
So long into the mysteries of Death—
My gaze had grown too dizzy ;—pained, and dazed.
Yet, though not scatheless, dauntless was I still ;
And unto Fate I cried Not Death ! not Death !—
I am baffled ; let me but turn round and look
As deep into the depths of Life ; for me
They can have nothing terrible : What can awe
One who hath stood before Eternity
With questionings and defiance ?—I would prove
The mightiest forces Life can bring to bear
On my untempted soul ; would test the pangs
Of sharpest anguish which thy will perverse

Can wreak upon a rebel 'gainst thy law ! . . .
Life ! henceforth be thy banes and blessings mine ;
Let me then touch thy gifts, so long disdained,
And see if they shall turn to curses now
For me, who dare to seize them recklessly,
Paying no tribute to their ruler, who
Demands as homage what my spirit free
Refuses, on its individual strength ;
Bearing no talisman to turn aside
The potency of their strange influence
Which, guided by some force inherent, claims
The lordship o'er the soul, to make or mar,
To raise it, or subdue ; to form—to quell. . . .
My soul would try her prowess with thee, Life,
In single combat ! . . .   So, alone, unwarned,
I flung myself into the tumult fierce
Of the wild storm that sways humanity.

And I made good my boast.   Did I not walk
By precipices, trembling not to fall ?
Did I not on the pleasures of the hour
Stake unscanned periods of consequence ?
Nay, did I not, for transient impulse, risk
Life-long regrets with calm audacity ?
. . . . But Fate hath iron chains, for those who thus
Resist her yoke ; vast their circumference,
Yet 'tis unbroken ; and the dooméd one
Who in vain confidence would spurn restraint,
Deeming his course unshackled—finds at last
How they inextricably close him round :
Relentlessly they fall across his path
Perhaps just where he swoops with headlong speed

In triumph of his orbit's boundlessness.
. . . And I! for laughing Fate to scorn, must learn
With what stern mockery she can repay. . . .
Thus hath her order been avenged on me,
Proving her sovereignty upon my will.
I was not left in singleness of soul
To bear my colours through the conflict hot. . .
O Life! *thy* mysteries were too great for me!
The darkness of the abysses infinite
Of the unknown—caused not my gaze to quail;
But in these complicated mazes, where
The end was hidden in illusive mist
And no less the beginning—all confused
I strayed, and lost myself in finiteness. . . . .
. . . . His being fell within my being's spell;
His life lived into mine. . . Alas for me!
I looked with dazzled eyes, and saw it come
Within the range of my sad spirit's gloom
And hover fearless o'er me—the bright-rayed,
The beauteous, the transcendent—it was *Love.*
Love, the sublimest blessing. . . O pure love!—
To me it came in guise of direst curse.
My soul, so shrouded in its dark despair,
Should have been all impervious to that light.
Why was I not more resolute?   Why not
Closed I my eyes, and hid them from its glare?
O! it was not for me!—I knew too well;
I put not forth my hands exultingly
To draw it without shudder to my grasp,
That blessing;—but I let it pass me nigh,
And linger trustingly in my caress—
Instead of shrinking from its presence blest

As should polluted feet from holy ground;
I let that all-surpassing radiance shine
Full on my eyes; which, for that one swift flash
Whereon, undaunted, they estatic gazed,
Must evermore be darkened hopelessly.
I gave myself up to the fleeting charm,
And drank of its intoxicating draughts,
And learned its mystic symbolism, and grew
Initiate in its secrets; took my fill
Of its brief bliss. . . . There was no warning voice
To check my mad impetuosity—
No gentle touch to hold me back.   For what
Were right and wrong to me?   Had I not learnt
To look on them as vague, and arbitrary,
Standards of unfixed value, wavering
Before the scrutiny of Reason bold?
O'er me they boasted no authority.
Repentance I disclaimed; and the mere name
Of evil was no fright to me; it had
No absolute existence; it was but
Acknowledged in the human systems frail
Which I had searched and tried, and cast away
In bitterest dissatisfaction.   Nought
Could they afford to my incessant plea,
My craving for some clue to certainty. . . . . .
I had brought many a wrong on my own head,
And warped and strained my faculties, and turned
Into the current of most innocent joys
The springs of fatal and accursed regrets
By my rash strife to wrest unto my good
The evil that might lie athwart my course. . . . .
Why not assert my boundless soul-claims now,

And try my spirit's force against the ban
Prohibiting all heavenly source of joy ?—
And so, I dared aspire unto the heights
Where the ethereal radiance glowed intense,
And was absorbed by it, and in its flush
Had my transfiguration. . . . . Vain ! in vain !
The sacred temple which I have profaned
Is shut against me ; and I wander now
Desolate, in the dark, without its bounds,
Doomed to eternal hungering and thirst
After the rapture of its hallowed rites !

I did not pause to count the cost. . . O God!
The immeasurable consequences !—How
In that bewilderment could I see clear ?
The risk was infinite.—I staked it all—
All, on one moment's madness. For I knew
I should but hurt myself : on me alone
The harm would come that ne'er might be undone.
He should go forth untrammelled on his way
After the brief indulgence of a dream
Which soothed his spirit with respite of delight—
While unto mine 'twas revelation of doom !
His life should be hereafter blest: for him
Were weaving happy ties of worldly peace
Which I would seek not to entangle.—I
Would never throw my shadow o'er the light
That goodness beamed around his future fair. . .
. . . I bound my curse more closely on my soul,
And vowed, in agony of expiring joy,
It should not compass him.—O sacrifice
Of love to love !—Upon my oath I took

I

The sacrament, in poison. Though it burnt
My lips, yet true in my heart's depth I keep
Its consecration still inviolate. . . . .

We did not say Farewell. . . We thought so soon
To meet again,—and if it had been so ?
He wished to be my better angel ; Nay,
In spite of me, he would be.—And what if
That had been possible ? . . Nay—nay ; such thought
I must not dare ; my mind is no more free.—
The inevitable doom came on us both ;
Fate took me at my word : my solemn vow,
She held me to it, most religiously.—
My prayer that he should be absolved—alas !
I know not, was it heard : there haunteth me
Like a vague horror, the anguish of the doubt
Whether *he* feels the meshes dragging him
Into their intricacy—limiting
The freedom of his chosen soul-career :
Whether his future is all sullied o'er
By the associations of that past :—
Whether his spirit sickens neath the blight
Once breathed on it by contact with my curse.

We are parted, and for ever. I am left
To bend beneath the unaverted load
Of my appalling destiny. The weight
In secretness of soul oppresses me ;
'Tis mine no more to struggle with it : now
If I would yet assert the hero in me
That will not be crushed down nor trampled out
—It must be by impassive fortitude,

Silent acceptance of my curse ; no more
I wear it openly, and wrestle free
In soul-assurance.   But through my despair
I cling to that proud consciousness which yet
Unshaken holds me with a strengthening grasp,
Beckoning still, as it hath done of old,
My spirit's course amidst the dangerous paths
Which menace with abysses horrible.
I have dared, and *borne* the wildest shocks of Life ;
Have dashed myself against her forces dread,
And am not shattered.   Still I stand erect,
And cry to Fate, "Thou mightier than I,
To thee will I not yet subject myself.
I have not fallen before thee : do thou still
Hurl after me thy vengeance.   I endure
All the results, though, with thy malice armed,
Of my unguided, irretrievable acts.—
But in this conflict I am none subdued,
Not more than in my futile enterprise
Against the mysteries of the unseen.
This is as hopeless. . . .   Yea, and I have paid
As dearly for my daring.   Death and Life
Are leagued against me. . . I *do not* succumb."

But ah !   Sometimes my victor-boldness quails ;
All my defiant courage lieth low,
And I, deserted, prone as passion's prey,
Sink in an agonising, whelméd sense
Of insupportable torture.   Then I wail
For the lost joy that never was my own—
All the more dear for what it might have been—
Then do I long to change my lot ; to escape

The pressure of heroic destiny :
I long to comfort me in my strange grief,
And weep for pitifulness ; long to feel
The sweetness of love's sorrow—not alone
The bitterness of this abandonment. . .

Then comes a meteor-thought o'er the deep gloom
Of my obscure soul ; then a faint-flashed hope
Lights through me, and dies.—*If there should be,*
    beyond
The sphere of this material universe
Preliminary (yet continuing it,
As the creations which men postulate
From elements chaotic, through the strife
Of their unwearied forces working out
Modifications inexhaustible
To climax of development)—*A world*
Of perfect re-adjustment, clear accord
Of impulses with opportunities—
A world that yields unintercepted scope
To the conjunction of affinities,
And perfecting of capabilities,
Released from the supremacy of doom.—
If that dim-comprehended, grand idea
Of blessedness conjectural, were a state
Where this same consciousness should be renewed,
And personalities come forth again
Each with distinctive attributes endowed,
Each unto other recognisable
By the soul-impress all indelible
Of character, immortal as the Truth—
And we *should meet once more*—How would it be ?

May I take comfort in that thought?—Will he?—
Nay; or his thoughts must cease to be, as now,
Holy: his holiness must ward from him
The haunting whispers which would keep alive
The lost love that he lavished once on me.
His life for lack of it will feel no void—
Rather, discumbered, its completeness reach
In glad communion with the good and blest.
He need not be drawn downward to the earth
By frenzied memories of temptation sore;
My vision need not come before his soul
To bar its flight unto his heaven of thought.
His aspirations soar—away from me,
Beyond the region which we mutual trod. . .
O'er them has my contaminatiou failed.
His *heart* was mine—I was magnanimous
—Rather, perhaps, I was most impotent—
His soul was left in freedom.   That I knew:
—We never might be joined in holy bond—
He was as 'twere a god, apart from me
Though he might stoop to me—O, gods before
Have stooped to rashest maidens, who have sinned,
Who, having lost all good, all hope of earth—
Have yet presumed aspiring unto heaven,
And deemed to dare sacredest heavenly joys
Earthly-weak!—with impunity: and theirs
Has been the fate, the punishment now mine!
. . . .   So do I read their lesson:—else there were
No meaning in the glorious olden myths,
The holy symbolisms that speak to us
Of the soul's deepest secrets, through the signs
Of beautiful religions, with their awe

Of nature's mysticism, their living might
Of spirit penetration.—So I feel
How utter powerless was my brief strength
In its infatuated bravery
To cope with his brief weakness; to o'ercome
The impelling force of the divine in him
Howe'er obscured, and unclear manifest
By my gross presence. . . . . O! he never was
He could not be—he never will be mine!

And dare I wish that he should think of me,
His evil temptress?—What was I to him?
—That I shall never know.   For him, 'twere best
It all might be as though it had not been.
For me alas!—it never can be so.—
"Do not forget me!"—No: love can betray,
Can mock, can murder—but *cannot* forget.

OF MY POET.
A Maiden Phantasy.

I KNEEL before a portrait: and I gaze
Immeasurable moments of still awe;
While the majestic beauty of the brow,
The far outstretching gleam of the deep eyes
Whose glamour, whose unearthly lustre, speak
Even from the motionless mute picture there;
The harmony divine, the wondrous power
Of the noble features, in their silence strong,
Their grand, sad pensiveness—sink in my soul
And permeate it, as I fondly deem,

With essence like as of that mighty soul
Whose motions once to such a mortal form
Gave life, and beauty, and a visible place
Amongst things tangible.   He, who is now
An inspiration, by his memory,
By his ethereal presence, in the spell
Of kindred thought, of deep-felt influence
Shed in the strength of his immortal words
Over the wide of all the ages—he
Moved once, amidst his fellow-mortals ; he,
Subject unto their frailties, bound and barred
By spirit-compelling chains of accident ;
Change, mood, the world—all tossed him in their
      sport,
From stage to stage of varying episode,
He lived the life with nameless men ; he paid
The tributes of all mean and little lives
Exacted. . . . . He was touched, was looked upon
By jostlers journeying on their few years' rut
Dragged in the limitless fields of Time—which he
Skirted, to clear them for Eternity !—
He was :—and *this* was he. . . . I try in vain
To feel that I am sure of it, and keep
Its firm conception in my constant mind,
Reiterating ever—" Thus he looked—
Just so."—Until I know the face by heart.
And yet, with each renewal of the look
I have some change to find, or, finding not,
I grow distract, and realise with rage
The incapability of painted stuff
To give presentment of the spirit form,
To speak with truth of living lineaments :

Then sometimes rebel thoughts, most passionful,
Surge up, and take possession of my will,
Crying—O, had I but been born, and died,
Before his actual form had passed from earth !
Alas ! I live too late !—The worth of life
Is only in the conscious privilege
Of sharing his humanity with him,
Of being called to the same mystic strife,
Of being steeped in self-same rhapsody,
And in its understanding partial
Being taught by slow degrees weak to conceive
The coursings of the essential soul in him.—
But why should I, who know this, and who feel
The nearness of the spirit-tie that waves
Between us o'er the unspaced labyrinth
Of the invisible—Why should I be doomed
To live apart from his identity,
Remote from farthest echo of his voice,
From lingering sign of bodily certainty?
O ! had I lived in contact with him blest,
Had but the rapture of such interchange
Of speech, and look, and touch, vouchsafed to me
As to the wayfarers who, heeding not,
Unmindful of their high prerogative,
Were near to him, in long companionship
—Walked side by side with him, yet felt no dread—
Thrown by a thousand turns of daily life
Into association intimate
With his soul-breathings?—Wherefore was not I
So happy?—O, to have poured out to him
All that is hidden in my soul—that must
For ever stagnate in its undrawn depths

Wanting the magic beck to charm it forth !
—O, to have made him look upon me once !
To have treasured everlastingly the tones
He flung me careless, in some passing chance
Of meeting—some requirement imminent
Of courtesy. . . . Or what if there had been
A closer bond ? And we, intuitive,
Had found the likeness and the waiting love
In one another's spirits ?—For I know,
It is—I do not dream it ;—all my life
Is not in idle fancy fashioned so
To sympathy with his ;—but there must be
Some likeness—some calm possibility
Of union in our souls : . . . And had we met
—As my dream-daring loves to figure me
With glorious audacity, that once
Hereafter, we *shall meet* in absolute life ;
Traversing mutual that eternal vast
Of being which may spread beyond our sleep—
Pacing, in intervals of chaos-dance
Or resting-pause in flings of searching whirl
Through universe-paths, the arcades of stars ;
Threading the milky way for infinite hours
Together, in a passionless lover's bliss—
New, self-immersing, passing all delight—
In ravishment so spiritual and pure
As to out-scope hot heart's intense desire. . . .
Sweet madness !—Ah ! that were a heavenly scheme,
Renounced with madness, and with dreams of heaven !
—But he has been on earth :—And if on earth
We might have met—Earth-heaven ! . . O, had we met,
How eagerly had recognition sprung

From each soul secret !   All the want of mine,
And all the depth of his sufficiency
From his ; how had the immediate kindling woke,
And we had been united, each to each
Indissolubly, of necessity !
My adoration perfect satisfied,
And he in the adoring utterly
Perfected, and fulfilled, and manifest. . . . .
But this is frail Faith's wavering.   I should be
Filled with all satisfaction, but to know
That he has lived ; to breathe the breath of life
That he has beautified, and made more true,
More real, more vivid, more sincere to me ;
In that his life is life for all mankind ;
Is life which is life's sparkling diadem,
Blazing with brightness through the looming dark
That would extinguish deeds and thoughts of men ;
Is life which sings clear-voiced to reverent Fame
Life's hymn—the pure hymn of life's sacredness !
His loves, his doubts, his passions, and his dreams,
His griefs, his wrestlings, his dark hours of pain,
His glooms of spirit-wrung despondency—
His terrible misgivings—live for us :
His light streams o'er the eventide of time
In undimmed glow of glory ; his great heart
Whose throbs of giant pain are hushed to peace,
Is beating through all hearts that throb with pain.
His trances of ecstatic godlike joy
Infuse our ecstasies with joy of gods ;
His lightning visions lambent flash athwart
The darkening dense of our drear dreamlessness ;
Our sorrow in his sorrow finds itself

Throned, and seer-sceptred, and with amaranth
  crowned.

His life was as a mournful symphony
Whereto all plaintive melodies are set ;
Whereto all passionate improvisos wild
May fling themselves, and into cadence fall ;
Whereto the impetuous throbbings of tense chords
Of yearning humanness may harmonise.
His wailings—as of those most sensitive strings
That palpitate with every faint-stirred wave
Of the impulsion of a dying sound—
Utter quick responses to the low notes
Struck sympathetic, to their melancholy.
Entrancing intertanglement ! weird-blent
Discords, to whose unjarring resonance
Diminished harmonies from every surge
Of passion's broken phrases, from the crash
Of agonisings in tempestuous shrieks
Concentrate, from the heavings and the gasps
Of the soul minor, rush into accord !

O ! it is good to live, and know that he
Has lived ; O, it is good for me to bask
In contemplation of that being, that once
Has been ; and shall be ; and for me still is.—
And, having been, makes being mine to me ! . . .

My thoughts, all uncontrollable, strain up,
Escaping from me in perplexity—
And when they utterly have gone from me,
Left me bewildered, me to seek in vain
To follow on vague traces of their track,

To seize some clue that may recal them to me,
Or bind to the remembrance of their sway
My after thoughts . . . then have I solacement,
Then do I know that they, my precious thoughts,
My priceless ones, my lost ones, are not lost,
Though lost to me; I know that they are gone
On their proud path, their unimpeded way,
Gone on towards his, gone up to meet *his* thoughts,
His thoughts which, all embracing, deign to stretch
To their reception :—his sublime, great thoughts
Eternised, ever hover, ever float
In the infinite :—So all the straying thoughts
Of the travail of our mortal anguish throes
Must meet in them, must be absorbed in them,
Must be resolved in their grand unison !
O ! and those omnipresent, almighty thoughts
Diffuse themselves over all time, all place—
They come to me, they reach down even to me ;
And when they cannot lift me up to them,
They make me all content to be abased ;
Make even my degradation glorious,
By being compared unto that altitude,
That unapproachable majesty of theirs !
—O ! there are moments in the which, to feel
How we, how all the day-dwellers of earth
Are crushed into one common nothingness
In presence of the ineffable magnitude
Of those, Time's great ones, is such supreme bliss
That the mere revelling in it raises us,
And makes us transiently inspired, to know
That this our littleness, contained in them
(Because their greatness all of us contains)
Is magnified ; is taken up into

Their breadth of being; we are great in them
As they are great for us; the many small
In the one greatness thus becoming one
Lose both themselves and their own littleness,
And in the universal are—what I
May be—nay, am, as often as I fling
My soul in its excessive rapture, far
From consciousness of all external things,
From meditation of vicissitudes,
Of earthly consequences, hourly cares—
As often as I drink the unsating draught
Of realisation of his realness,
His veritable intensity, his force
Of soul pervading—when I feel so full
Of the glory that I share in being one
Who can commune in his communion free,
And in his open fellowship have joy,
That I do feel his presence, and his power,
More than in universal;—I do feel
That he is *mine;* as though he had but lived
To be my antetype; to echo back
To my heart-cravings satisfying cries;
To be reflection for me of the needs,
The wonderings, inexpressible by me,
And ne'er for me by other to be expressed,
But only by his potency:—meseems
As though the far-off life he lived on earth
Amongst his peers, removed from influences
That now determine the allotted course
To every struggling pilgrim of *this* age—
As though that life had but been lived apart
For me to live into; a life for mine
To find a refuge in, from this chill life

That spreads around me—strange, unreal to me,
I cannot find myself therein ;—it seems
The essence of my life has been hid in his,
And only as he will distil it to me
May I partake of it :—O, it does seem
My life is his, he is my only life,
And in his life am I, who could not be
Without it,—he interprets uuto me
All that I feel, or know, or wish, or dare ;
It is through him I long ; through his delights
I recognise my own ; and through his grief,
Surely, I suffer ; with the self-same pangs
And quiverings. . . .   Only, where I lay me low
And abject, that the storm sweeps over me,
And the fell victor passion treads me down,
And I succumb,—and even at last may grow
Resigned to the invincible anguish, . . there
He conquered ; he has borne aloft for me
The standard of man's splendid might of will ;
And over life's woes and heart's frailty, high
It fluttereth, triumphant evermore.
. . . Ah, glorious one ! in every onslaught dread
Of world-foes, of opinion tyrannous,
Of slander, treachery, arbitrariness,
He breasted all the fury ; stood his ground
With foot firm, head erect, and brow unstained.
He did assert victorious liberty,
Did vindicate his pure soul-royalty—
He was the unfailing champion of the true,
The noble, and the fearless, in the race
Of man inherent ; Manhood, fallen alas
Unto most vile abasement, is in him
Dignified, raised unto its lofty height

Of privilege, of empire, and of pride. . . .
O beautiful !—*that* wert thou to the world,
That was the plan stupendous, and the end
Of thy most blessèd mission.   But to me,
What wert thou ? . . . O ! what art thou !
        . . . . Thus, my heart
Floods unto him. . . . . It is more pure than love,
More mighty, more divine than ought can be
Which agitates the passion fleet that men
Call love, and glorify, as though it were
A force of exaltation. . . What it is
Never as mortal do I long to know ;
I am content—nay, not content ; for such
Serenity as in contentment dwells
Is not compatible with this strange glow
Of ardent zeal . . yet will I say, content ;
Content with my devotion ultimate,
My one aim, my absorption, my intense
Fill of existence. . . . I will call it love,
Since I do know no other name on earth—
And that name never shall be desecrate
By being turned aside to lowlier flame.—
Unto no living one shall my quick pulse
Quicken, no eager flush shall fire my cheek
Nor wild pant check my breath, at sudden dart
Of spirit communication, at swift word
Of unvoiced message deep sunk in the heart,
From one of these, the pigmies of my race
Who now surround me—while my soul is vowed
Unto the worship of the immortal one,
The deep-revered, the long-loved, faithful loved
Of the great dead—the chosen of my soul,
Its true ideal—my one love—my own !

" CHANSONNETTE."

If life might all be dreaming,
  And ne'er a dream might fade ;
Or all be real that's seeming,
  How blissful life were made.

If but the golden future
  Might e'er " come true " to me—
Or that sweet *past* come back again,
  How beauteous all would be !

To live in that dear waking dream
  My soul were all too blest ;
And weariness were charmed away,
  And longing—ah ! at rest !

EVEN OUR FAITH.

O ! THE dearest thing to lose is that which was never
    possesst ;
For all that has once been ours is for ever and ever
    our own ;
The lightest touch that has lain on our hand leaves
    trace of its rest ;
We feel it again, when we will—its impress for us
    alone.

The one good-night that was said in a voice we shall
    hear no more
Says itself over again in each waking watch of the
    night,
Lulls to the sweetest of sleep, with a spell that was
    never before
In the hushing words oft repeated of tones familiar
    and light.

But nought that has given us reckoning—of our joy,
    our longing, our trust,
Is so sacred as that faint wish that could not be
    measured in life,
The uninterpreted omen, that ne'er was made good,
    that yet must
Hover deep on our spirit's depths to touch and allay
    their strife.

K

The mystic, ecstatic strain at the bounds of rapture, that went
  From the ken of the soul, leaving after a need never understood ;
The striving towards bliss too far, that its force on the way all spent ;
  The aimless, the wild devotion to the improved invisible good :

The vision that has come to us, when we closed our eyes from the light,
  Then opened them full for sure gaze, to find it vanished and fled—
The day offers things that are real, day after day, to our sight ;
  But we choose to return to the darkness, and cherish its dream instead.

.   .   .   .   .

O, the false love is dearer, dearer than the true, though it come at last ;
  It rules, usurper ; it cannot vanquish the soft regret
For the meteor charm eclipsed unfulfilled, that un-challenging passed
  Incomparable ;—no memory like that which we *should* forget.

No promise that hath its reward can render us half the grace
  Of the vague, the beautiful hope that flitted, faded away

Insensibly, ere it was questioned, the mystery that
glancéd in our face
And was lost in the height o'er our head, in the flight
that no wonder could stay.

A wound that is made can heal, more sharp or less
though it be,
And the deeper or the less deep by a different scar
is shown ;
But the pain undefined, too wide for a place, draweth
constantly ;
No sign: but in every part a nameless sickness alone.

We drink at the cup of yearning, but never may have
our fill
Though we drink ourselves mad; we pour out our
heart on deceptions sweet,
They fail us, our faith is spoiled without reparation ;—
and still
We sigh for them possible.   No disillusion is quite
complete. . . .

. . . . And the Truth that we feel our way to by
treacherous guesses alone
If we reach we can grasp it not, feel not its evident
place at our side,
Nor manifest even to ourselves its presence—nor let it
be shown
To the world, waiting, how the *fair lie we have wor-
shipped is Truth that has lied.*

THE PHILOSOPHER TO HIS DEATH-POTION.

DEAR draught of Death !   Sweet salve to sense !   How
    do I welcome thee !
Dearer than potent love-philter, sweeter than sweet
    to me :
Welcome, to lips that oft have thirsted as they thirst
    not now,
With fervid thirst that never draught of life can quell
    as thou !
I have drunk madness from the bowl whence glows the
    sparkling wine ;
Drunk deep from many a languid cup a lassitude divine;
But the transient spells have failed to soothe the rage
    that raves in me—
That can alone the lasting languor that I seek in thee.
The intoxication of one passionate moment, made eterne,
Can satisfy alone the longing fires that in me burn.

Life hath itself its opiates ; thereof I have quaffed too
    deep ;
I have known too oft the listlessness of their ecstatic
    sleep :
Oblivion's trance luxuriously hath closed my eyes in
    peace—
O ! the blissful sense of soothing brief which bade
    sensation cease—

But O! the waking agonised ! the shuddering shock,
    the change
At the reopening of the eyes upon the old, yet strange
Life dreariness :—the sickening new revulsion, the
    cold thrill
At finding when the dream was fled the darkness
    clinging still ! . . . . .
. . . . . . My last hour ! My last moment! Now
    the life that was in me
Hath surged itself quite out. How oft from unreality
I have been startled into realness ; hurled, with awful
    power,
From cheat of dream-bliss to the dragging of the
    cruel hour :—
And now—I scarce conceive—scarce dare believe this
    certainty—
The bless'd prospect scarce can yet be realised to me ;—
To think, that no to-morrow now can bring me more
    the pain
Of opening eyes upon the struggle back from sleep
    again !
O ! wild anticipation ! Beatific ecstasy !
Rapt tremor of delight, absorbing as infinity !
O whirl of exultation, seizing on my reeling brain,
Dashing its frenzied eagerness beyond the grasp of pain !
O, glory of bliss ineffable !—To feel, it draweth nigh—
It comes—it shall not shrink from me again—to die—
    to die !
O mystery ! . . What sudden flash may gleam these
    eyes before,
Dazzling them past all vision, ere they fade for ever-
    more—

What paroxysm of intense sensation—what sublime
New consciousness—what subtle combination—fusion
    of time
With the eternal limitless—what wonder—what swift
    glow
Of perfect knowledge soon must rush on me—how
    may I know?
—What shall be mine—or what excess of clear ideas
    —what plain
Presentment of those verities that speech can ne'er
    attain ;
What fulness of the inexpressible, rendering satiate
The flooded faculties. . . . I know not.—Brief the
    space to wait
Ere all reveals itself to me, victor by Eternity
Of the secrets in life's silence hid. . . . I once, un-
    reasoningly
Demanded energy perpetual—sought, with storm of
    strife
For exercise of all my force—some elixir of life ;
But now, for that vague indeterminate energy, mere rest ;
An absolute lull in my conflicting forces, deem I best.
—To pass, with all my possible powers, at one sur-
    passing thrill,
One effort grand, into quiescence utter—that I will !

    .   .   .   .   .   .

Strange, how in its last moments this my personality
As it hovers over nothingness—about extinct to be—
Keeps its very vivid consciousness—asserts its innate
    power
With importunate insistance, strong as in life's earliest
    hour.

. . . The soul that will annihilate itself, how can it be
In the instant of transition, all that now I feel in me ?
What is it, that seems swelling with a thousand
   powers combined ?
Instinct with thousand impulses, extending infinite mind ?
The gathering up of all that ever was, or is, in me ?
The seeming germ immutable of all that yet shall be ?
Full with forebodings that might stretch to reach
   Eternity,
With nascent quiverings that would seem beginnings
   of to be ?
. . . . Is it transmutable, indeed, into the latent store
Of faculties which shall renew the race for evermore—
The universal force, unconscious of identity,
Waiting to be called forth to individuality,
Ready to be resumed into an active state again,
As the fitful energy breaks forth, that long has dormant
   lain,
When some modified conditions find it change of
   scope anew ? . . . .
Is this life principle within my being as sure, as true ?
Is it imperishable ?—Does its nature still remain
In the wondrous conservation all unchanged ?—Does
   it retain
Potentiality infinite ?—Or may it die away
Exhausted with successive cycles, as the sun-force may ?
Or can it be crushed out without indemnity ?—effaced
As the transient prints on melting snow, the lines on
   water traced ? . . .
Wonder inscrutable to itself is this humanity ?—
How long have I impetuous asked myself, What now
   of *thee*

I ask—solution of the mystery; answer full and clear.

No more delusions I accept ;—I seize the answer—here!

.   .   .   .   .   .

Ah! often in the pause of the slow, toilsome, waiting
  years,

With tears whose mockery hath recalled memory of
  holier tears,

The passion of a wish has come on me—the wild
  thought stirred

With frantic fire my spirit's torpor :—"Ah! had Heaven
  but heard

The prayer that I in childhood breathed, that I a child
  might die—

Ah! little comprehending then!—Alas, the unwitting
  cry—,

What prophecy it uttered of the manhood's foredoomed strife—

What instinct filled it of the undivining dread of life!

Why did not God believe me?"—in its bitterness hath
  said

My heart, when writhing consciously in that fulfilled,
  full dread.

How have I longed to call back from the depths of my
  past peace

That blessèd childhood!—go back unto that, and with
  it cease ;

How have I longed to lay my head upon its innocent
  breast,

There close my wearied eyes without a thought and
  take my rest.

What rapture, then, to recognise, now I no more can
  pray,

Requital of that prayer, whose yearning ne'er hath
    passed away!

All that I once have had, and lost,—of joy, of love, of
    thought,
In spirit-presence for one moment back to me is
    brought;
All that I have been, now *is* me; what, but an hour before
Was severed from me by long years of change—is
    mine once more:
Fairest youth, with all its fairness;—e'en pure child-
    hood's purity;
All the ardour long burnt out, the fancy lost,
    revive in me;
Those past moments I have lived through, in the rush
    of passions rife,
When life lived into one moment, and one moment
    lived through life—
How long since their vitality has faded !—But they
    blend
With the actual moments of this later selfhood—at
    its end,
Now *these* moments, charged with present individuality,
Verge on to the one extinction where all quenched
    alike shall be,—
And the past becomes the present—for the present is
    the past.
All life's moments reuniting in one moment—that the
    last!
The one moment of solution, wherein all of life doth lie—
Moment brief of comprehension—present—past—
    futurity;

When all that hath been, all that e'er might be,
    participate
In the swift passing of one moment's being concentrate

.   .   .   .   .   .

Now even the meaning ceaseth of the very memory
Of the anguish whence deriveth all my life's intensity;
It has come, at last, the ebb of all vibrations of desire;
'Tis the ultimate cessation of the passion-feeding fire.
No feeling pulsates through me more; regret is all
    gone by;—
I envy not the happiest ones who ne'er have longed to die.
No looking back disturbs my blissful calm; no
    tremulous doubt;
All changefulness, all vacillating fear, are now died out;
Nought know I of remorse:—the wrong, the sorrow
    of my lot,
Not unremembered, but effete as though remembered
    not;
The stumbling in my ended course—the slipping . .
    ay, the fall. . . .
The signet of necessity is stamped upon them all! . . .
Even on this final action:—to the general harmony
Of the universe, it sways obedient.—This is what
    must be. . . .
Farewell, fond contemplation!—All engrossment
    now be o'er—
Heil dir! beloved death-bringer! . . . I pledge thee
    —ah!—*no more.*

SHADOW AND FORM.

'Tis true that there is nought to be desired,
Nought, save desire itself: if that were lost
All that seems now so beautiful, ungained,
Would become loathsome, and a weariness.
Possession sickens—ay, of the rarest joy.
If we could have all granted and assured
Whose search makes life one eager, rushing race,
For which the imploring cry raves through the world,
Reaching past Heaven, and finding never bourne
To arrest its course impetuous—were it so,
Then life were nought, and there were nought beyond.

. . . . "Victory, or the abbey !"—cry inspired,
Inspiring !   All the might that greatest deeds
Of warfare, wonderful accomplishment
Of skill and courage, of success, required,
Worked in the spell of that alternative.
. . . But it was figured merely ; its effect
Most real and true—its promise vacant, void ;
The trusted compact with posterity
Utterly disregarded ; the proud hope
So strong with the living, to the sacred dead
Unrealised. . . . Were the aspiring words
Only vain, futile bubble-blowing of speech ?

Nay, their immortal spirit hath a truth
High and mysterious, that lives on in act,
In will and in intention, in ideal
Personal, national, cosmopolitan.
Let not presumptuous reason of man demand
Stuff to oppose unto the verity
Of the unmanifest, ethereal
Substance : . . . it were as fond, as laughable,
As 'tis to ask of science render count
Of the soul's essence—in psychology. . . . . .
" Victory—or—" Well, it was victory,—
For our interpretation glorying ;
He could not have its consciousness, and yet
The sweet sense of the mystic unfulfilled,
Which is at the heart of all our longings deep.
" Westminster Abbey !"—The reproachful voice
Of surface sentiment, the railing loud
Of overweening, satisfied, yet slight
Perception of fitness—cry out in disgust
That the fair symmetry of the recompense
Is marred, and retribution frustrate made.
It is not so ! O, earnest readers all
Of the law beneath the letter—O ye know
It is not so. The spirit is fulfilled
Of that sublime adjural ; as must be
Spite of all contradictions obvious
Ever the spirit pure and absolute
Of influence-working charm or prophecy.
O ! reverent lovers of the deathless dead,
Can ye stand in that silent emptiness
Midst all the monumental mockery,
And feel that by the mouldering dust beneath

Our glorious dead are represented best?
That they whose past selves are the legacy
Of the survivors, selfless living out
On the memory of their identity,
Are best unto their fame associate
By the records of these walls? Do not your souls
Bear record otherwise? Do ye not feel
When most by your religious ecstacy
Subdued, and in fit frame for consort pure
With the unseen presence of the form divine
One, manifold, that lendeth glory and awe
To the columned cavern of Godhead—feel ye not
That *he is there?*—He—not his relic bones
Beneath the age-trod aisle-floor casketed ;—
But the prophetic cry, that was at once
Life-pass and epitaph of the soldier soul,
Is in the holy, the fame-rustling air
That sanctifies the precinct stones, enshrined !

Did not the dying Bruce bequeath his heart
Unto his faithful vassal, with the charge
To bear it, fighting, to the Holy Land,
In the soothing faith its last rest should be there ?·
How was the wish fulfilled? More lavishly
Than ever mortal could fulfil design.
Unto the bearer of the sacred pledge
The unthrobbing heart was more than mightiest spell
—Sovereign salvation of his dear renown,
Incitement to most godly-daring deeds.
He never reached the sweet goal of desire,
But died, o'erwhelmed with glory, in the trust
To which his death was faithful. . .   Then that heart

Was carried sadly back to Scottish soil,
And laid to rest in Melrose Abbey walls. . .
And to futurity it was bequest
Of the most noble poem, which has dwelt
Unwritten, but not powerless, in the souls
Of all who hear the legend, all who muse
Upon the mighty destiny of that heart
So far beyond its boding—ay, beyond
Its hottest wish, its most exultant leap.
And they who cherish the remembrance grand
Of that pathetic story—if they think
Of the ruins where the burial hath been—
Must needs surrender to the inward voice
That cries " O gallant heart ! *Thou art not there !* "

What is accomplished shows what may be done,
What is projected only, shows what *might.*
The ideal that remains but in idea
Loses not its first brightness, nor in aught
Is from the perfect pattern derogate ;
That which is carried out must suffer and fall,
Submit to compromise, and be pollute,
Descending from the far-off throne where high
It stands, a model for all time to come,
A wonder, and a worship.   That which is
Can never overpass the boundary
That limits it from the unattainable
Of that which might be, that which should be.   Look
To that, and ye are lightened ; turn away
From the apparent—find the hidden real.

EXPERIENTIA DOCET.

"The little fools !"—we wise ones say ;
Seeing how they rush onward to their ill,
Seeing our sage words, our dear-learned counsels, still,
How they are thrown away.—

Rash ones !—before your eyes each day
Pass not examples of the truth we tell ?
Only experience sad can teach you well,
And—then—"Too late !" you say.

And yet our warning we repeat,
Discouraged not, in hope to find, some day,
But one who timely may be turned away
From that fell poison sweet.

"Touch not, O taste not !—though so fair,"
(To the deluded ones we earnest cry)
"That lovely fruit ye hover longing by—
Its knowledge is despair !

"It is the fatal fruit, so sweet
At the first eager taste ; but evermore
The tempted one shall rue that moment sore
When he did take and eat.

"For all too quickly is he cursed;
The sweetness into bitterness soon turns,
And leaves with him a sickening pain, that burns
With an enduring thirst!

"And once that harm is done, no more
Can ought be found that may be remedy:—
Think of the long, sure suffering, and pass by.—
The joy were briefly o'er!"

—In vain: we still entreat in vain;
The wild infatuation urges on
The reckless ones to snatch the sweet;—'tis gone—
The bitter doth remain! . . .

There comes a voice from out the crowd
—Victims of that dire curiosity—
It breaketh in with strange audacity—
It crieth out aloud—

"Yes! it is even as you say—
We, who would not be warned, did seize and eat,
And by the bitterness after that sweet
Must we our boldness pay.

"And yet, for all the after pain,
We would not that enchanting sweetness first
Forego, for knowledge of the lasting thirst,
If we might choose again!

"We would not pass untempted by,
And live, not having known the taste; nor yet

Renounce the bitter, if we must forget
The sweetness past thereby.

" We know not how—but it is so,
That after revelling on that bitter-sweet
We would of no more dainties henceforth eat,
No other sweetness know.

" We never now could find our bliss
In aught of the delights which yet remain
To those who have not known the joy, the pain,
That we have lost in this.

" One blessèd moment only stayed
The gladness ; but our very life is left
Changed by it ; and we would not be bereft
Of that whence it is made ! "—

Alas !—then you must go your way ;
There is no saving from the treacherous snare,
No power of help, no wisdom to beware,
If that be as you say.

If that indeed be all the gain
Your fatal knowledge unto you hath brought,—
If that be wisdom by experience bought,—
Such wisdom is in vain !

We wise ones need not lift our voice—
Let folly cry, and be held back no more,
But teach the world its lesson, as before,
To sorrow and rejoice ! . . . .

L

AFTER SUNSET.

. . . . . . Hast watched the sky
Tinted with evenings brightest, fairest hues,
To greet the solemn passing of the sun?
Seems not all Nature in that mellowed light
To grow more fair? and gentle eventime
Shedding a softened halo o'er the earth
To make its beauties seem more wonderful?

But—when the sun has gone from the fair west;
And the last streak of glorious, radiant hue
That heralded his flight, has passed away;
And the bright lines of golden, seeming lit
With wildfire from his dying majesty,
Have faded from each cloud's resplendent marge;
While from his chariot part the tints sublime
That gathered from the crest of each far hill
To lend a glory to his dying hour
And usher it out with pomp of kingly state;—
When the soft shades of silvery eventide
Have deepened o'er the mountain's gloomy brow:
And the last glimmering brightness leaves the sea,
Where twilight shadows are creeping; and from the
    wave
Is yielded sadly in the rose-tinged foam

The last fair beam reflected in its glow;—
When the proud monarch, verging to his fall,
With one last effort of superb command
Gathers together all the lingering rays
That faint unto the advancing gloom of night,
And marshals them, in deep mysterious gleams
Of parting light that roll along the sky
Till they unite in one grand canopy
To mirror on the darkening sky (with gloom
Too soon to be obscured) the shimmering hues
Whose brilliancy late flooded those pale clouds—
When the translucent tints, that floated o'er
The fleecy flecks, absorbing them utterly
In their pure lustre (they, ardent with mystic glow
Transfigured gleamed one moment, to melt in light)
—Have faded from the heaven's dull leaden hue—
Then—then—draws near the dark and dreary night !

O ! when thus evening waneth—hast thou sighed
That those sweet charms should pass within an hour
And mourned the fleeting beauty now no more ? . . . .

Watch ! Seest thou not, far o'er the mountain side,
Parting the dark folds of yon heavy cloud,
A gentle star steal forth upon the night ?
Watch ! . . still !—So silently—and scarce perceived—
Star after star shines out, . . . until, ere long,
The heavens are gleaming with their awful light—
And space seems widening to infinity.
The restless struggle—the change—the uncertainty—
Seem sunk into the far past ;—nought can stir
The stillness of this serenity ; no jar

Subsist against this blissful sense of rest.—
O ! doth *this* spell not call up in thy soul
Joy yet more sacred ?   And inspire in thee
More noble thoughts ?   Seems not thy spirit then
More great, more powerful ?   And this gloom to be
More worthy of thy reverence and thy love
Than evening's transient, mocking loveliness?
Now that hath passed, with its delusive shows,
How sweet it seems to turn, as in relief,
To this grand emblem of enduring calm :
How changless, and how imperturbable
Its glory !—how deep, how holy its repose !
Ah ! Night can give more peace unto thy heart,
And wake sublimer powers within thy soul,
And breathe into thy mind more blessèd themes,
And teach thee how with Nature to commune
In higher and more hallowed intercourse—
Than day, with its bright sunlight ; or its close
In sunset splendour, and brief beauty of change.

Thus, in the darkening night-time of thy grief,
When turns thy soul in anguish to that fair past
But late with all its joys, its visions bright
Of supernatural glory, parted from thee :—
When from thy life the illusive light is gone
Whose glory beaming o'er it had made it seem
Too beautiful for true, flooding it o'er
With loveliness and radiance all unreal—
Then shall Heaven send a pure, still light, to gleam
Through thy deep darkness ; and that light shall bring
Far clearer revelations, visions more true
Of the mysterious spiritual things,

Than the departed bliss of thy regret.
And, in that blesséd light, thy soul shall be
Lift up toward that far brightness gleaming ever
Beyond the horizen dim that bounds *our* view.

TROTH.

My recantation !—No, that cannot be !
'Tis not within my will.   O poetry,
My love of life, my life of love ! to thee
I am bound for ever.   Not at prayer of mine
Was the glorious boon acceded to me ; thine
The choice, the search of me.   O my divine
Sovereign, my perfect mistress, at the voice
Of thy first movement in me, I did rejoice,
Before full comprehension of thy choice :
With awed unquestioning reverence, at thy feet
I fell, with vow of true obedience sweet,
Ready thy absolute behest to meet.

To love thee unrequite were ecstasy,
But now thy gracious recognition to me
Hath come—now may I ever worship thee
In calm, full, strong assurance—O my God !
     O Poetry !

EMBLEMATIC.

Fate plays Parrhasius with me :—not as he,
That olden painter, for art's sake pitiless
With bodily torment had his victim racked,
That to the world he might bequeath the work
Won from the expressive throes of dying pain,
Snatching from transitory agony
Its soul of beauty, to delineate
In art immortalised beatitude. . . .
Not from such suffering might in me be found
Material for the artist of my race :—
But 'tis my very soul that shall be torn,
Heedless of my brief anguish ;—rent to shreds,
In disregard of rebel impotence,
Or the tremendous, yet all futile strain
Of effort to endurance : 'tis my soul
That must in present moments be convulsed
Beyond capacity of my frail powers
So grasp with comprehension resolute. . .
But so it is, that in some wondrous way
Tis sacrificed unto futurity,
This soul, whose quiverings must some purpose serve,
Known only to the master, who doth use,
His mystic power upon it ruthlessly.
Henceforth its very tatters may be kept

For long elaboration by his hand—
The potter's hand, that moulds his plastic clay
Into sublimest symbolism of form,
Regardless of its substance loathliest,
Serenely, through its writhings of effete
Unorganised resistance, firm and calm
Persisting, till his absolute design
Subdue, transform, transfigure the yielding stuff,
To the perfection of the finished work. . . . .
I in a potter's hand am clay—*but clay* ;
And ere the master-spirit, that on me
Worketh his will, hath raised me to such height
Of glorious probability—'tis need
That I have been degraded, in the mire
Trampled and crushed. . .   Nor can I hope to share
The triumph of the after perfectness
Of the ideal to be wrought forth in me ;
Since 'tis the workmanship, and not the clay,
That owns the beauty and the blessedness,
That serveth to the glory and the joy
Of coming ages ; and that doth endure
To immortality, when the vile stuff
Hath its identity complete absorbed
Unto extinction, in the form divine. . . .
Poor grovelling, transient, unregarded clay—
Despised, indeed ; let it be still despised
And lose not its humiliation, till
Past recognition it become endued
With the divinity, transmitted once
To its base medium—for Eternity.

THE DREAM OF LIFE.

LIFE, and not death, to me—seems like a sleep ;
Which, in a lingering dream—successions fleet
Of changing dreams—faint consciousness doth keep.
So . . . . childhood is the first fair, blissful dream. . . .
And youth—half-waking lapse, where all things seem
Still tinted with th' enchanted light that fell
O'er that pure, lovely vision ; and its spell
Hath power to lure the fancy, that, dreaming on,
Seeks still to mingle beauteous dream-forms gone
With its confused, awaking sleep ;—and so
Youth's dream from child-dream's light hath caught its
    glow.
For so celestial beamed—so clear—so bright
The glamour of the yet scarce melted light,
That fain the uncertain sense would deem it true,
And struggles not to lose it quite from view ;
To frame the visions of its after sight
Unto similitude of that blest light.

So life dreams on.—The fitful, broken sleep
Youth's hopeful vision may not ever keep—
To manhood gliding, whence the light must fade
Of the bright images, whose beauty made
A glory, which at first so real did seem,
To hover o'er the passing of the dream.

But now no more those charms around it dwell ;
No more, obedient to sweet fancy's spell,
The thronging forms their wasted likeness keep :
But, lost in a perturbed and restless sleep,
Dark, fearful figures dim flit to and fro,
—Shapeless—confused—uncertain—come and go.
The dreamer holds no longer 'neath his sway
His dream ; nor hath he power to bid it stay.
Not vivid visions, seeming-real, and clear,
Delude him now :—a vague and helpless fear
Burdens the trance-bound spirit ; and o'er it steals
A strange, uncomprehending awe, that feels
A boding of the moment *to awake,*
Which soon, with dreadful shock, must sudden break
The spell of these illusions ; and leave, alone,
The horrible darkness, with its depths unknown—
The nothingness in which all being must end—
Of which a doubtful consciousness doth blend
With the yet wavering sense, that strives in vain
The ever-fading mockery to retain.

One moment of dread transition ; and no more. . . .
The horror of that bewilderment is o'er.—
From fettered sleep the waking soul unbound
Conscious assumes her glorious powers new found ;
Grasps the full comprehension, fearlessly,
Of all her being's awful mystery ;—
Into herself all force of life receives,
And all its grandeur, all its truth, perceives. . . . .
The dream is broken—in reality !
The soul from life's sleep awakes into Eternity !

·　　　·　　　·　　　·　　　·

Then sees the spirit, how that fair dream of yore
That faded slowly till 'twas dream no more—
Was no delusion ; and its transient light,
That dimmer ever grew to earthly sight,
Was but a faint glow of celestial gleam,
Shed erst o'er childhood, whose imperfect dream
Such a conception of that light attained
As might by mortal senses be retained ;
Whose beauty as a shadowing-forth should be
Of the soul's true and heavenly destiny :
And the fair likeness in that dream dim traced
(Ne'er from the darkening spirit quite effaced
That deep and deeper into the gloom must go,
And mist unpierced by that ethereal glow)
Must only then, at last, forgotten be
When realised in most blest certainty :—
The sweet dream lost but in fulfilment ; past
All changing maze, all fleeting shows, at last
To the freed soul opens Eternity ;
Where, far transcending all thought, all prophecy,
The infinite source of that pure light revealed shall be

ONLY A COQUETTE.

Only a coquette !—So winning, and so sweet,
—So innocent, I read her.   Was I blind ?
Did she not to me show, even despite herself,
The secret goodness of her deepest soul ?
It is there—or it has been :—I am sure,
Too sacred for the jeering world to see
Into whose conventions she has fallen bound ;
They only ask her brilliance.   I, who felt
The truth in her, o'erlaid by all those lies
She glittered in—I would have laid it bare,
Have vindicated in her, for her sake,
The noble nature in her—had she would
For my sake, for my love's sake.   Wanton fool,
Hovering between the choice of Heaven and Hell !
She stopped the string of the yearnings that I touched,
Whose motions, had they had full way allowed,
Had swept space with the infinite vibratings
Of the natural chord,—successive reproduced,
Echoing, faint, faint, distance on distances—
Whose ground-note, ere 'twas muffled, I struck true
That moment when her eyes drooped, and her lip
Struggled 'twixt sweet humility and scorn,
Before I said I loved her—when I asked
If love might not be better than the crowns

Of adulation, and the triumphs gained.
O'er all the envious, who could but avow
That she was beautiful. . . . Might it not be
A sweeter victory to know herself
Not to the world, to one, one only—*dear?*
Ah! had she answered then—because no speech
Framed itself to the tones so apt to dart
The lances keen of wit and arrogant play—
For that I know, the silence gave consent;
And half the moment owned that she was won.
It was but half a moment.—Then we burst
Upon the crowd, into the lights and flags,
The rustle, and the distant music and stir. . . . .
Not an hour after, and I saw her pass—
I, watching for a dropping glance to fall
On me, who waited in the corridor,
Wrapt in my blisful musing, unaware
Of the fling around me, and the flying feet.—
She saw me not; her eyes were fixed upon
Her cavalier;—he closer to her side
Than I had been in my soft murmurings.
Those two seemed listening to each other's looks;
She gazed up to him—he was very tall—
As though her eyes would drink from his. Her smile
Was mournful, but derisive hauteur loomed
From her white brow. I heard the words she spoke.
. . . "I find that there is surfeit of all sweets;
Of all things one may have enough too soon
—Even of freedom—even of fun: indeed
One can grow tired of being young. I do.
My life is not so good to me, that I
Love not death better; nay, I think that now,

Having run through all enjoyments, only this
Is left me to desire for novelty :
And any moment I were grateful, glad,
That death should come and take me by surprise ;
I would not cavil at it for its lack
Of ceremony—chide it inopportune.
If at the end of this next valse—with you—
My heart might in one instant cease to beat,
I would not ask for warning ; would not stay,
Not for one mundane sigh, for one regret,
Not for one lingering starlight air adieu,—
Not for one last sip of champagne ! " . . . Was it *she*,
Who turned the humour with such flippant words ?
She, without change of gesture or of mien
Drifting so lightly into scoffing strain,
Availing her of her too versatile
Mood-phases, thus to blazon to the view
Of the unreligious, of the stranger, who
" Not intermeddleth "—her immortal pains
In alternation with bright repartee,
Soulless by contrast,—swiftly, easily,
Gliding o'er the transit, as indifferent
To the difference ; and all to amuse herself,
To strike, to startle, to bring out, to try
The last acquaintance of ten minutes' stand !—
O ! could I then have spoken ! Could I but
Have intercepted—with an earnest speech
That should have caught and checked her levity——
But he, the coxcomb, eager-drawling, snatched
The opportunity to dawdle out
Loudly a compliment !—about the strange
Reversal of the usual privilege—

The unlooked for probability that she
Should fall at *his* feet, ere upon his heart
He might make bold to lay her.—Scurrilous fool,
And sneaking cynic!—O, she did not blush!—
As her light dress trailed past me, from her hair
A spray of flower detached itself, and fell
By fluttering stages, from the gauzy scarf
That swept her shoulders, to the hanging lace
Entangled in the girdle of her fan
—Thence flung from the frail tassel to the floor.
—I stooped me after her to drag it up—
Only to find its debris sparkling there
Crushed and dispersed—down-trodden by the heel
Of the swaggering partner. So I heard no more
How the word-tournament pursued its course,
Nor how its end might tally with its grave
Solemn beginning. And I had not time
—Or will—or common sense—in thinking o'er
The sudden revelation—to feel shocked,
Indignant, at her wild, unmaidenly
Impiety. I only thought, with thrill
Of passionate sympathy—"Then she is sad!
This life of change, of outward gaiety,
Is not enough for her; she takes the whirl
Of inclinations, part ungratified,
Part sated,—at its value; turns from it
And looks beyond it, giddy. . . Dreary queen,
Tired of her joyless kingdom! Sick of power,
Sway-weary!—Ah, she knows not what it is
She needs; but I have found it for her: would
I could persuade her to believe it! then
Accept at my own hands the unfailing cure;

Be satisfied, and rest; yield and be glad;
Know both the want and its fulfilment, both
In one—taught in one moment, in one kiss!
'Tis I will do the deed; 'tis I will be
Her teacher, her inspirer ; I will place
The nectar to those dry lips, that through smiles
Of stoicism ineffable, are hot
For thirst with which the unheaving bosom burns.
. . . She can be melancholy ; she who deigns
To lay aside her cold serenity
For sport with merry mockers ;—who can dress
Tormenting thoughts with phrases light and gay,
And in sad cadence utter trifles fond ;—
Whose lightsomeness betrays heart-vacancy ;
She pines : she knows not—but I have the charm
To kindle her young life to glory : *love!*
I have love to bring her ! . . by that need of it
She hath, who needs nought else, yet, needing that
Hath all the rest too little—she shall be
Love to my love. My love for her. She *is mine.*" . . .
Audacity exultant! Joyous thought !
Undoubting aspiration !—I could smile
Now, at my own simplicity. Belief
Is very true, and can suspect no guile.—
O ! I can think of it no longer !—Wrath
Hastens me on. . . . One flash of memory
Shows me my siren in that farewell hour
—I did not know it was farewell; I thought
It was the first when my new Paradise
Should open to me, and receive me lord
And rightful owner ;—me, who long without
Had dwelt, in adoration of close gaze.

Ah! had I but held back for evermore,
Gazing and feasting on the loveliness
Free unto me as unto all men then,
Who were content to be outside and gaze.
O! I drew nearer: and was yet not near
Enough; would enter in, and take to me
Of its delights possession. . . . Ah! . . *that kiss!* . . .
I had dreamed my life away in it, for hours
Of wonder, of anticipation. . . Fool,
To make such trial! After all, perhaps
My test was wrong: it failed me wretchedly.
. . . I stormed her in one fervid, seething kiss,
Hoping that she would pale, and that her awe
Would faithfully betray her love to me.
But her cheek quivered not; and she looked up—
In my arms—turning on me most dazzlingly
Her dark, superb eyes; and in them I saw
A calm, clear laugh, in tearful moisture hidden;
And her caressing, silvery voice sobbed low
Untrembling—" Ce n'est que le premier pas
Qui coûte."—O shame! then mine was not the first!
—It cost her nothing; she was used to it.
. . . . She told me afterwards, when I adjured
Her tenderness to me, by memory of
That one embrace, that I so sacredly
Meant, loyal;—told me that a kiss, to her,
Was a mere physical sensation; said
" That one thing as another must be good
To kiss, so it were flesh:"—A girl's, those words!—
I think she had learnt the new philosophy!
It was, I found, the kind, fraternal mode
Of her admirers all to greet her so.

M

Surely it must have palled upon her ! stale
Even then ; how wearyingly it must have grown
Unto her custom !—O how many arms
Have wreathed around her since ! how oft her head
Has laid itself sweetly on other breasts
In condescending dalliance, as with me then !—
—She, tossed from one to another, at their will,
Not caring—she, who should have had my love,
And been my angel.   What may she not be
Now ?   Has she fallen, at last, from the proud height,
The perilous precipice whereon she played ?
Or only gradual bent, more low and low,
Till she is now as much beneath the need
Of man's protection as of his real love ?
She, who disdained the one, must surely be
Bereft, at last, of both—faithless to both,
Worthless. . .   And yet—she was so much to me !
She might have been so good ; she was so fair :—
She had been gentle. O, what could it be
Made her degraded, wicked ?   Is there ought
Hath such a devilish power o'er woman's soul ?
Yes ! vanity !—profane, mad, merciless
Vanity ! Ah, we know that—we, as men,
Know what it is ; but not what it can be
In woman—in its empire over her.
She is its slave—endued with terrible might
Lent to her by her master—vanity !
'Twas that which made her listen to me, take
The flattering words I offered to her face
Like all the rest who thronged around her ; all
Had learnt the dialect, and came with lips
Twisted to false mock-vows, which I in truth

Took; and they pleased her equally from me
And those who travestied.   Truth was to her
No dearer than a lie ; and she doled out
Exact to all, mixed meed of truth and lie. . . .
No more of her !—she is not for my thought—
" Guarda e passa !"—Only a Coquette. . . .
She is done with, is she not ? Then that is all!

AHNUNG.

Out of my sorrow, that dieth,
  Come great gladness, that shall live ;
The joy that grief purifieth
  Be mine—not to have, but give.

Into my loneliness enter
  The lives of all that shall be ;
In my thoughts unspeakable, centre
  All motions of sympathy.

For the slow, sad present, that fleeth
  And the fair past, fled—
Be mine the far future, that seeeth
  The durance of all bliss dead !

SESAME.

Love is a moment's mastery : its strange spell
Is worked by chance coincidence most slight
Of episode and mood—of thought and sight,
Of touch and impulse.   Ay, as sure, as well
The magic power effects its sorcery
Within one pulse-beat—as in years of foredoomed
    energy.

A voice, deep, sweet, low, sympathetic, heard
In the sudden when soul-music through the still
Of the inward secret trembles ; and the will
Is stretched in longing to be answering stirred
By swift perceived accord.—Such voice must be
At such conjunction of the spirit forces—destiny.

One word, one smile, one whisper, one caress—
Enough : the enchantment binds the captive fast.
Into the unsearched darkness of the past,
Through all the intricate of the wilderness
Of circumstance, of influence unknown,
Of the life long hidden, quick revealed, the new-roused
    thought has flown.

Rash thought ! patient as strength, as instinct bold,
It follows out the associations far

—The most remote—of that strange life ; there are
No clues to the present that remain untold.
Every dim feeling, sign too faint to last—
Interpreted ; transient expression caught ere it hath
    passed.

And not the past or present alone can be
Thrown into light by passion's instant glare
Unto perception perfect ; but its share
Claims the illuminate thought, audaciously,
In the farthest reaching future.   Every right
Of love is won—or missed—at once, at love's first
    stroke of might.

TO "FEU MA MAÎTRESSE."

My sister heard from you the other day :
   In her letter, a message for me
Included—*your kind regards :* I may
   Take myself so much flattery :—

You remember me, at least.   But how ?
   No more than the words imply ?
No otherwise ?—I might well by now
   Have passed from your memory ;

—That I was quite prepared for ; long
   Since you threw me over ; 'twas right
To have done with me so :—but O ! it is wrong
   To hold me in thought so slight.

.   .   .   .   .   .

Have I forgotten that summer day ?
   Not I !—I wonder, have you ?
In the glorious woods that you chose for play,
   When you fooled me—and loved me, too.

Out of the sunlight, in the cool shade,
   How sweetly were secrets smiled !
How easily meanings whispered, vows made,
   How charmingly hearts beguiled !.

You loved me, me for myself, all me,
  Though you loved so many more ;
I understand now how that can be—
  Not then :—had I known before !

Or perhaps you were not yourself at all ;
  Did not show for just what you were,
But acted a part, as you would at a ball,—
  You, the actress everywhere !

O ! you should have thrown off your tricks, your wiles
  And softened at nature's spell ;
In the air was not radiance more than your smiles ;
  And love seemed in both, as well.

And I, when I found me at your feet,
  Seemed so in my natural place ;
I could wonder not, in the presence sweet
  Of the glamour of your face.

   . . . . . .

Keep of me what remembrance you will
  —Though I rather would say, Forget—
But if any it be, be it earnest still—
  For I, what I was, am yet.

And if you know that 'tis I indeed
  Who all that long time ago
Flung my soul to you in its trust and its need—
  How you tossed it me back you know.

How you had your way with it ; how you took
  For use, what you would of it ; then

Went on your way with a scornful look
  —No thanks—not a smile again !

That was well, if you would I should be no more
  To you—'twas for you to will ;
But nought could be hence as it was before,
  —You cannot be you to me, still !

Send me no words :—call not back the past ;
  Do not venture a doubtful claim
On associations of old, at last,
  In friendship's, in memory's name.

You were all, or nought to me ; I to you
  Cannot be what you want of me,
—If you mean to waste me and have me too :
  I tell you, it cannot be !

UNREST.

The song of a weary pilgrim
Beside Time's fated strand,
Dooméd to tread the mystic track
Whose end is hidden, which turns not back,
Through the shades of a dreary land.

"O ! my soul is sick and weary ;
My feet are tired and sore ;
My journey is lone and mournful—
Shall I wander for evermore ?
The way, so long and tedious—
I know not where it may tend ;
Will it never lead to a pathway ?
Shall I never find the end ?
On, on I go ; but all vainly ;
My feet lead me round and round,—
Must I thus stray for ever ?
May never a *rest* be found ?
O ! vain and unanswered longings,
Will ye ne'er be calmed to peace ?
O ! pilgrimage sore and dreary,
Will never thy anguish cease ?"

Forth chanted, bitter and wailing,
Monotonous, dull and low,

Came from life's path the echo
Of that sad plaint's ceaseless flow.
And the pilgrim, with this dark burden
Of unrest upon his soul,
Wandered through Fate's stern marches,
And knew not they had a goal !

There came, then, a vision to him ;
And a voice spoke, sweet and blest,
Answering in his soul the strife,
The yearning, the long unrest—
" On ! on !—Fate hath appointed
A journey drear for thee ;
Thou canst not thread its mazes,
Its bourne thou canst not see ;
Steep is the path, and rugged ;
'Tis vain to hope for a rest
Till thy destiny be attainéd
And thy journey ended, blest.
And though, whilst thou faintly toilest,
Thou knowest not where it tend—
Press on, untiring only—
And thou shalt achieve the end.
Still struggle bravely onwards,
Till there come in sight—*the goal* ;
Then the sweetest sense of restfulness
Be granted unto thy soul.
All the blissful realising
In one transient moment's gleam
Of the restless, troubled yearnings
That shall fade away as a dream.
The weariness, care, and sadness

Fall from thy spirit away,
Sinking in long oblivion,
Lulled into peace for aye.
Then the tedious journey is ended—
Not a weary step o'er again ;
To this end they have all been leading—
The anguish, the doubt, the pain.—
. . . . Wake ! put on all thy vigour ;
Stretch forth with all thy strength ;
No more unanswered questionings ;
—Trust—hope—thou shalt find, at length ! "

As the sleeping trance passed from him,
And the day-light greeted his eyes,
The waking senses came rushing
With an eager, glad surprise ;
And he felt, in his new sweet blessedness
As though the fetters did fall
That so long the soul had burdened
That fretted and chafed at their thrall.
And an energy, strange and *hopeful,*
Fired in each nerve and limb ;
And a strong resolve woke in him,
—His spirit awoke in him.

Forward he went ; nor ceaséd
The painful path to tread ;
But O ! how many dragging years
The gloomy journey led !
The sweet hope ne'er quite failed him—
But O ! how oft it grew dim,
When the same unrest and fearfulness

Perplexed and weighed on him.
How oft he longed, impatient,
But to lie down and rest ;
To give up the dreary pilgrimage
And its far-off bourne so blest !
But he paused not ; and ever onward
Wandered, with failing strength,
Till his weariness gained upon him—
He must give up, at length !
So faint grew his limbs, and weary,
He scarce could tread one step more ;
But until that promised bourne appeared
How might his journey be o'er ?
He struggled on :—then, powerless,
He fell to the earth, at last—
But the pain, the aching, the tiredness,
Were passing from him fast. . .
And again, as though he were trancéd,
He heard the sweet low voice
Whose call he so true had followed,
Whose tones bade his heart rejoice—
" Rest ! thou shalt go no farther—
The goal that thou couldst not see,
That, seeking, thou still hast hoped for,
Is here appointed thee !
No mark for thine eyes discerning ;
It might not to thee be known
Where the end was doomed to the pathway,
Thou hadst trodden in pain, alone.
No rest on the way was given ;
But the languor, that at last
Came so strong, and overpowered thee

Was sign that it all was past !
Now, the rest so long denied thee,
Cometh, unsought, to thy soul ;
Rise not—no more shalt thou wander—
This, pilgrim, is the *goal.*
For ever—and ever—and ever
Sleep on ; all peaceful and blest ;
All care—all longing—all weariness
Lulled to eternal rest ! ”—

And the Voice all gently faded, ...
And left him—still and calm :
And a sweet sense, his soul pervading
With peace, brought a wondrous balm.
His spirit all thrilled—filled
With ecstasy, pure and blest. . .
All laid to sleep, the longings
Unanswered, the wild unrest ;
One moment of rapture, passing
To dreamless, unmoved rest.

. . . .

All life long was his pilgrimage,
And in *death* he reached the Goal ;
And the *rest* he found,—shall come, at length,
To every weary soul.

FRAGMENTS OF THOUGHT.

ALFRED DE MUSSET—AND UNE AUTRE.

Sorrow, too, hath her worshippers. A voice
Cried once unto the Gods for a great grief.
The prayer was answered. Unto him whose choice
Was made so strange and awful, came a brief
Exquisite rapture, first, forcing his soul rejoice. . .
Fatal, delusive, treacherous !—The spell
Was of love's madness cast, to purpose bent
Of the heaven-courted fury, which swift fell
Upon the insatiate suppliant. Thus was sent
The crowning anguish of joy's quick life.—It was well.

And there was one who wearied her of rest,
And sickened of the joy she ne'er had known,
And put its vision from her. To be blest
She asked *better than happiness* alone ;
Not bliss, nor hope :—but more : and it was granted
 . . . . Was it best ?

NOUS AVONS CHANGÉ.

BLEST forgers of the noble myths of old,
The trust, the reverence, the piety
Of those dear beauty adorers, patriots bold,
Priests, poets, pilots of humanity—

Mild, pitiful, was their most gentle creed ;
Not ours : for they unto their Hell assigned
Their Lethe : we are soothed not so :—indeed
It is in Heaven that we must Lethe seek—nor Heaven
    without it find!

HERZENSBLUTTROPF.

Long had I to keep a treasure, whose dear worth I did
    not know.
Alas! I guarded it carelessly—and too soon I let it go.
Now it is lost to me, deem I it all preciousest things
    above :
And I love it for aye, with a sorrow that is greater
    than even the love.

PLASM.

Of no life should the standard be success.
How should it be?—Not each one his own fate
To fashion hath ; but all the lives to bless
That his can comprehend—or touch. The world can
    wait.

THE END.